ANDREW

LANNING'S LEAP BOOK 5

Kathi S. Barton

This is a work of fiction. Names, characters, places, and incidents are products of the author's imagination or are used fictitiously and are not to be construed as real. Any resemblance to actual events, locations, organizations, or persons, living or dead, is entirely coincidental.

World Castle Publishing, LLC
Pensacola, Florida
Copyright © Kathi S. Barton 2016
Paperback ISBN: 9781629893839
eBook ISBN: 9781629893846
First Edition World Castle Publishing, LLC April 4, 2016
http://www.worldcastlepublishing.com
Licensing Notes
All rights reserved. No part of this book may be used or reproduced in any manner whatsoever without written permission, except in the case of brief quotations embodied in articles and reviews.
Cover: Karen Fuller
Editor: Eric Johnston
Editor: Maxine Bringenberg

PROLOGUE

18 Months Ago

Laci looked in her rearview mirror and let out a long sigh. Finally, her aunt was asleep. She wasn't sure how much more she could take of her maiden aunt traveling with her, but she'd not been able to leave her behind and Laci wasn't sure that either of them would have survived had they not had each other to depend on. Not that her aunt was all that helpful, but she was her responsibility.

The trip — it had really only started out as a small trip — had been to go to the market. It had turned into a nightmarish run across the states. That had been eleven days ago. Much longer than she wanted to think about moving so far from her job, her home, and everything she'd left behind. But there wasn't any way for her to stay there when people were trying to kill her.

Laci had arrived home that day to see her aunt sitting outside of the house in her wheelchair with her pocket book on her lap. Not a purse but a pocket book. She needed to run into town for a bit. Just to pick up her prescription, she'd told Laci, and a gallon of milk. Laci had no idea how her aunt drank so much milk, but every day her aunt would either have her pick some up on her way home or she would meet her, as she had that day, ready to go get it. More often than not, even if she called home to see if there was anything her aunt Jeanie needed, they'd end up making a trip out of the house to get milk and just one or two other things.

The store had been crowded. The holidays were over, but it was the first of the month. Never a good time to go to a store, and certainly not a good time to be out and about for any reason. Her aunt Jeanie never cared if Laci had to park in the far lot. Her chair was her throne, and she didn't care how far Laci had to cart the groceries.

Laci remembered thinking that she was glad then that she'd cashed her check. Aunt Jeanie got her pension each month, but as far as Laci knew she never spent any of it. Certainly not around the house for things so mundane as food and power, anyway. Laci was paying for everything, including her aunt's medical bills that her insurance didn't cover, as well as any personal things that she needed. Laci was making it each month, but it had been getting harder and harder to make ends meet. Then they'd gone to the store.

The cart was being pushed around by her aunt in one of those electric chairs. Aunt Jeanie loved it, Laci knew. Riding around without having to struggle with her wheels on her own put her in a particularly good mood that day. Laci also thought that her aunt used the time at the store as a social thing, being that she pretty much stayed at the house while Laci worked all the time. They were just rounding the canned vegetable aisle when the cart stopped moving.

"Is it the battery?" Laci had no idea and said that to her. "Perhaps that's it. The battery. Go and find me someone that can change it out, or you can go out and get my own chair. I need to be here for a bit longer...to get the things that we need. You'll have to push me if you do that. We only need a few things."

"I'll find someone." As she eyed the cart with over a dozen un-needed items in it, Laci wondered how the hell this had happened every time. Each time they only needed milk, the grocery bill would amount to right around fifty bucks. It would be more if there were only a few items in addition to the milk.

Laci only wanted to go home, put her feet up, and take a short nap before she had to go back to her other job. Life was decidedly harder since her parents had died and she'd taken over the care of Aunt Jeanie. Laci made her way to the front of the store when she realized how quiet it was.

She was nearly halfway up the aisle to the front desk when she saw the two men. One of them had a mask on; the other was standing with his back to her. But he wasn't covering his face. It took her several seconds of just standing there to realize that he was holding someone in front of him and he had a gun to their head. Moving to the back of the aisle again, she never turned but backed up one step at a time, keeping her eyes on the two men. She needed to get to her purse and her phone where her aunt was to call the police.

"Going somewhere?" The blunt end of something touching the back of her neck had her stilling. The man, because there was no doubt it was a man, laughed. "Come on now. You want to join the party, don't you?"

"Not particularly." He hit her with the gun but only hard enough to make her see stars and not knock her out. Moving when he gave her a shove, Laci tried to think. "If you're robbing the place, you'd be better off just leaving the customers alone. The only reason that most of them are here is because it's the first of the month."

"We don't really care about the money. There is something more here that we're to pick up. A bigger pay off." She nodded and stopped when they reached the offices. "Stand still and I won't kill you right now."

The office, really just an open area that sat about two feet higher off the floor than the rest of the store, was full of people when she was shoved into it. There was a wraparound desk in it, a safe that was currently closed, as well as four people standing and three sitting with their hands on their heads. Two were bleeding out on the floor, and Laci could see that they weren't going to make it. Laci looked around for her aunt. Thankfully, she wasn't anywhere near here.

Laci took a quick inventory of the men holding guns. Two had handguns, one a rifle, and the other one was behind her still, and she knew that he had a gun but nothing more. The odds were too great for her to get brave, but that didn't mean she wasn't going to jump if the opportunity presented itself. She'd been trained in hand-to-hand combat, how to use a gun, and to know when to stand back and let the chips fall.

One of Laci's jobs was that of a security officer. The other two—one an antique buyer, the other a sales associate that sold grave plots to people—did not help her as well right now as the first one did. She knew the make and model of the gun, the kind of ammo it held, as well as how many shots it would fire before it would need a new clip. She also knew that it would do a world of hurt on anyone that was on the receiving end of it. Death would be about the only option should it hit you in any major part of the body. The man behind her spoke finally, and they all turned toward her.

"Found this one wandering around the store. I thought we put them all in the freezer. But here she is, right here just out in the open for us. This is her, right?" That explained the quietness of the store, Laci thought. But she had no idea what he meant by singling her out. "We got what we came for, so we can leave now, right?"

"I have a suggestion." She was hit in the head again. "That fucking hurt. Stop doing that and I won't have to hurt you."

He laughed again, which she figured he was justified in doing since he had the gun. Laci was tall, lanky, and looked like a good wind would blow her over. But she was strong, agile, as well as trained to take on the bad guys when necessary. When he hit her again, she'd had enough.

Grabbing his arm, she flipped him over her head and then used the momentum to jerk his arm around and snap it. As he was screaming at her, she used his own finger to shoot and kill the mask wearing guy and then hit the other one before he had a chance to fire back. As she ran for cover, shooting the man on the floor once in the head, she made her way to the back again.

Her aunt was just where she'd left her, sitting in the aisle with a broken chair. But she had a man holding a gun to her head when Laci slid to a stop at the end of the aisle. Laci had started for her when a bullet whizzing by her had her ducking for cover again. It more than likely had been the injured man from the front offices. Laci dove behind the meat counter just as the man with her aunt came after her.

Laci sat here, her back to the counter, and thought about what the fuck had just happened. Robbery. That was clear, but why wait until now, when the store was over crowded with people to pull it off? And what had they meant when they said that they'd gotten what they came for? Checking the clip in her gun, she'd nearly wet herself when one of the men laughed close to her.

"Laci? Where are you? Come on out now. We just wanna talk to you." Laci had thought her grandmother had given them her name when the man continued and wondered why she'd do that. "Come on now, don't make it harder on yourself. We know that you're her. Someone told us you were gonna be here, and damned if they weren't right this time. We kept missing you before. But I have to tell you, the lure of making some extra cash on this by robbing the place is gonna work out so much better for us. This way they'll think it a simple job, and the fact that you were our intended prize won't ever come out."

She had wanted to ask them what the hell they wanted her for, but she heard the sirens at the front of the store again. The men started cursing, and she waited there. One of them surely was going to finish the job. And when he'd come through the swinging doors at her, she fired four times before she saw him fall back. The police were the next to talk to her, telling her to drop her weapon.

"You should have stayed there and let them talk to you. Those men weren't gonna hurt you none." Her aunt was awake apparently and still fussing with her over things. "What harm could it have done you to talk to the police either? Then I'd not be sitting here with my ass hurting like it is."

"I'm sure that had they killed you, you'd be bitching about that too." Aunt Jeanie huffed at her. "The police were not who they said they were. I've told you that like fifty times already. They weren't cops."

"So you keep telling me. He was in a uniform, wasn't he? What else was he supposed to be?" Laci said nothing, the story too old for her to care to repeat herself now. "And now they're all looking for you and you're gonna drag me along with you."

"Thanks, Aunt Jeanie. I'm so glad that you care so very little about what happens to me. And I've told you, several times now, that I can drop you off anywhere you want. Just say the word." Another huff. "No? Then I would suggest, since you made me go to the store in the first place, that you keep your mouth shut."

It really wasn't her aunt's fault that those men were chasing her. But blaming her would keep her off her back for a little while, and Laci wanted the quiet time. There had been little to none of that as they'd set out on this mad dash for safety.

When she'd traveled as far as she could for one night, Laci pulled into a rest stop and parked the car. She was broke. All the money she'd had on her was now gone. Her credit cards weren't safe, not that she could use them with them all maxed out like they were. And Laci had watched enough television to know that not just the good guys could track that, but the bad ones as well. Until she could figure out what the hell was going on, she wasn't trusting anyone.

Closing her eyes, Laci tried to relax enough that she could sleep for a little bit before moving again. But almost as soon as she drifted off, she saw the face of the "cop" when he'd told her to kick her gun to him.

"I'm not going to hurt you, Laci." It had taken her almost too long to realize that there wasn't any way for him to know her name. "Come on, miss. Just toss the gun this way and we'll get you out of here before those men return."

"Will they?" He nodded and looked to his right. She couldn't have seen what was behind him, but she had a feeling that she might not want to know anyway. "Did you have back up coming? If so, I'd really like to wait for them."

"They're dead." He grinned at her when she asked him who. "You are too smart and that might get you hurt. Why can't you just do as you're told and come out of there and let us get on with the day?"

"I think you're not an officer, are you?" He shook his head and moved into the room, pointing the gun at her. "What is going on? Why are you looking for me?"

"I was just told to find you, kill you, and then bring your dead carcass to them." She asked him who again. "Don't know his name. But you're too valuable, he told us, to leave running around like you are. Come on now, you can't kill me. I've done not one thing to hurt you."

Laci had had a feeling that there might have been a "yet" at the end of his statement, but a sound behind him had him turning and her firing at the same time. The bullet had caught him in the shoulder, and he fired twice before she managed to kill him.

Laci opened her eyes when she saw the man's face in her memories, the neat little hole in the center of his forehead where she'd hit him. Calming her heart down again, she wondered what kind of prison terms she'd get for killing three people, all of them bad guys. She sat there, staring off into the dark, and tried to think what had made anyone want to kill her. Shifting on the seat so she could lie down, Laci felt the overwhelming urge to cry. Not that it had done her any good so far, but that didn't lessen her need to do it.

CHAPTER 1

"You bought a cable company." Andrew nodded, thinking that Phillip was going to make fun of him too. "And this cable company, it has a problem and you want me to help you figure it out."

"It has a lot of problems, but this one I want to fix on my own. It's failing. And I haven't any idea why anyone this day and age would open a cable company this small and expect it to work. I mean, I have a bit of a clue but not the whole story yet. That's where you come in." He handed him several sheets of paper. "Okay, see those numbers? Those are the sales records for all the people in the customer service department. The ones in the first column are from first shift, the other two for second and third. There is a weekend crew, but they only answer the phones and set up sales when asked. They don't actually go out looking for them."

"Okay. Looks pretty even I guess. I mean, I don't know shit about cable or customer service, but these look to be pretty good." Yeah, Andrew thought so as well. "What is it I'm supposed to be seeing that I'm not?"

He handed him another sheet. "These are the sales reports per computer. I hadn't any idea that it could be narrowed down that way. But apparently it can. Now look at the second shift ones."

Andrew had bought the company for the sole purpose of tearing it apart and using the building for something else. There was another company around that served most of the needs of the community for all their television watching needs. They even had phone as well as Internet. He used them himself. But once he started looking things over, he decided he was too bored to let this pass him by.

"They look like everyone is sharing the same computer. So?" Andrew shook his head. "They're not? Then why are they coming from the...? Ah, I see. You want me to go and find out for you. How did you want me to handle this for you, Andrew, spy on them?"

"Yes." Phillip told him he'd been joking. "I'm not. I've sent in a couple of other people, ones that work there, and they have no idea. I think it's more than that. Like one person is responsible for this and they're not fixing it."

"Why? Why would they do that? I mean, if they're getting paid commissions on each sale, why would this person not be keeping it all for themselves? To me, it looks like this person is sharing his commissions with his entire shift." Andrew said he didn't know. "Why do you even care?"

"I don't know that either." Andrew leaned back on his chair. "To be honest with you, since we closed up the search and rescue business I'm bored to death. I find myself listening to the scanner to see if Murph might need me to come and help her out. By the way, she might be a little touchy about me. I think I might have pissed her off."

"Yeah, I heard." Of course he had. And Andrew was pretty sure that the rest of them had as well if he had. "What the hell were you thinking going into her interview room like that? And then proceeding to let the man she was talking to think you were with the police?"

"I told you. I'm bored." He'd been screamed at for over an hour by her, threatened with arrest, and she'd told him she was going to tell his mom. That was the most powerful threat to him. He, like the rest of his brothers, were scared shitless of their mom. As he was pretty sure the women were as well.

"Okay. And I'm only asking, not saying I'll do this, but what is it you want me to do?" He grinned at his brother. "You already have an idea what is going on, don't you?"

"No. I mean, yes, but not really. I know that for some reason this person's sales are being shared with the shift. Sometimes even on other shifts. I can't find out anything other than the person's last name…is Summer. First initial is a B." He handed him what he had on the employee. "You'd be surprised at how little information I'm able to get from anyone. This guy, Blair Warren, the man who is helping me get my feet wet, as he called it? He said that the systems are forever down so he can't get me what I asked for. And every time I ask for a key to the filing cabinet, he tells me that I don't need it. I'm going to have to have a long talk with this guy before I fire him."

"He does realize that you own his ass, doesn't he? And if he's not playing ball, how did you get this?" He told him that Max had helped him. "And can he figure out why this is going on? Or is it another thing you want to do because you're sick of pissing off your sister-in-law, the town sheriff?"

Andrew thought about what he was doing. And why. He'd been bored, just as he'd told Phillip he was, but it was more than that. Andrew felt useless. Not only that, but he hadn't found a damned thing to keep himself from not getting into trouble. Not until this came up.

"I told her I was sorry and she said she understood. Then she told me if I darkened her steps again, unless I was being shot at, she might shoot me herself." Phillip laughed. "I have my house the way I want it. I'm educated, have money to burn, but I find that is just fluff. I need something to do."

"You want to go back to work for Rescue?" He told him no, not ever again. "Me either. I mean, I'm bored too. Not like you are because I have a mate, but I am sort of lost until we get that shop up and running. Charlie has her business going now. Mom and Hannah are enjoying working for her, but I feel like I've been set out to pasture. I've even taken up golf. Christ, I hate that shit too."

"So? You'll do it?" Phillip said he would. But only for a few days. "Thank you. So much. I just need to know. I will tell you that I might end up closing it anyway, but I just wanted to do something."

After his brother left, Andrew looked over the paperwork again. Max had told him that the systems were never down, nor did he see any reason for them not to give him access to the files. He knew that his nephew was holding something back, but until it became clear that it was necessary for him to know it, he wasn't going to let Max tell him. Andrew really needed to do this.

Two weeks ago they'd closed up their search and rescue business. It had been a relief really, to know that he'd not have to go out on those sort of jobs again. The search part of their job meant murders most of the time, and the rescue was never really any more than body retrieval. He had been burnt out long before Misha had asked them if they wanted to continue doing it. Andrew had his desk cleared out that same day and had gone looking for someplace to unwind.

It had taken him all of twenty-four hours to realize that he wasn't cut out to be a man of leisure. That vacations were not what he'd needed. And that the women that he'd dated in the past were no longer something he wanted. He had four of the best women in his family now in the way of sisters, and everyone else had failed to make the cut.

Leaving his house to meet up with Misha and two more of his brothers, he drove by the cable company again. He didn't go in but sat in the parking lot just looking at it. He had no idea why, but he had a feeling that something was going on there and he wanted to crack it. Smiling when he thought he sounded like Murph, he started his car up and moved to the restaurant. It was time for some fun.

~~~

Laci sat at her desk and watched the others get ready for their shift out of the corner of her eye. Really, getting ready didn't mean the same to them as it did her. She was working, they were bullshitting and having a good time. As she dug out her head set and the pens and paper she'd brought from home, she wondered what they were going to do when in thirteen days she was gone.

Giving her two weeks' notice had been hard. The job was paying the bills, yes, but it was getting harder and harder for her to come to this stupid job and not get the kind of money she was supposed to be making. They were ripping her off and everyone knew it. They thought—and she supposed rightly so—that she was a sap. But she was done with that too.

Her first check had been wonderful. The sales commission money that she'd worked her ass off for was going to make such a difference in their lives. It had amounted to well over what her hourly check had been, and she'd cashed the check and put a large portion of it in her

17

stash. If they had to run again, and that was a forgone conclusion, she wanted money to do it on.

Then her next check had come in. It was considerably less than it should have been, by hundreds of dollars. Most of her commissions were gone…no reason for it, just not on her check. Not only were they not on her check so she could get paid for them, but someone had gone into the computer and changed her name to those of the people she worked with on the work orders. She knew there had to be some sort of computer issue and had decided to talk to someone about it.

After getting in to her appointment to see her boss, Blair Warren — he'd canceled on her four times — she was seated in his office. Her entire shift of customer service personnel had been there as well. Laci had her sales reports in hand, having printed them up each night when she was done for the day, as well as a list of the names that had been changed to someone other than her. She thought she had been ready.

"You're a very good customer service rep. The best this company has had since I've been here." She thanked him, not sure what he was up to. "The rest of them, the others on your shift, can't even hold a candle to the amount of sales you have in one week. Not even if they worked for an entire month."

"Yes, that's what I wanted to talk to you about. Their names are on some of my sales. I don't understand…. Maybe we should do this in private." He just shook his head. "All right then. I have my nightly sales report for the week that this check should have covered. As you can see, there is over nine hundred dollars in sales that have been changed to show someone else made the sales. I was — "

"I know. I did it. So?" She could only stare at him, with not even a clue as to why he'd do it. "I don't see what the problem is. You make more than the rest of them and that's why I did it. And I will continue to do so. Had we had someone like you here years ago, even months, our business wouldn't be on the chopping block and we'd be able to compete with the other cable providers."

"But I earned that money." She looked around at the people in the room, all of them smirking and laughing. "Some of these people, they're the ones that you're giving it to. Giving them my money."

"Actually, all of them are getting a cut of it. Even me." Blair looked at them before looking at her again. "None of them have had even near the sales you've had. And a few of them, most really, have been on the edge of being fired for some time. When you came along, well...it seemed the only way to keep them was to make sure they had the sales they needed. Now corporate is happy, I'm happy, and it's not like you're not getting some of your money. Just not all of it."

"I'm not happy. Not the least bit." He'd laughed at her then. "I'm not going to do this. I'll quit first. Or report you. This is theft and you know it."

"Will you? I don't think so." He had nodded and the people filed out, most of them laughing at her still. When the door was closed behind them, Blair leaned back in his chair. "I know who you are. And that you're in trouble. I can pick up that phone right now and have you not just arrested, but that aunt of yours killed as well. How far do you think you'll get before you, too, have a bullet in your head?"

Her mind had nearly shut down. How the hell had he figured it out? She'd only been doing her job, not causing any trouble. He was stealing from her and thought that it was okay because someone wanted her dead?

"You're kidding me? You'd have me killed over money?" Blair had just stared at her, his face telling her that he would, in a heartbeat. "I'll go to your boss. Then his if I can't get any satisfaction."

"You'll never make it that far." It wasn't a threat but a hard cold fact. He would make a call. And then she'd be dead. And Laci hadn't a clue as to why they were chasing her. "Go back to work, Laci. May I call you that? Anyway, I'm glad that you're here, I have some rules to go over with you. You can't tell anyone about this, not the new owner, not the police, or anyone else that might come here and look into this. You slow your sales down, I'll call. You tell anyone, I call. If you so much as hint to anyone that you're being blackmailed, I'll call."

"This isn't right. You have to see that." He told her that it was his right to do as he pleased. "No, that's not fair. I worked hard for that money. I need it."

She'd left his office then, him not saying another word to her. That had been over five weeks ago and now she was finished with this stupid job. She still wasn't sure what she could have done then, any more than she was now.

"Hello." Laci looked up at the man standing over her desk and felt her body tense. All her mind could grasp was that he'd finally done it. Blair had figured out she was quitting and he'd called someone in. "I'm Eric Phillip. Most people call me Phillip."

"La...Beth Summer." He nodded. And when he continued to stand there, she looked around. "Can I help you?"

"You didn't get the email." Shaking her head, she explained that she didn't have email. "I mean here. You were supposed to get.... Never mind. I'm here so you can train me. I'm the new guy in this department."

This had to be a joke. Laci stood up and looked at the others. She wondered which one of them were playing a joke on her. Sitting down, Phillip handed her a copy of what appeared to be an email. She read it over twice and still felt like it was a terrible joke.

"I don't understand. I'm to train you? For this department?" He nodded, looking as confused as she felt. "I've never trained anyone before. I don't even think I was trained."

"Well, that's what it says." Nodding, she laid it with her things. "What do we do to start? I'm assuming that you have to get on the phones?"

"Yes. The phones." Taking the rest of her things out of her bag, she tried to think what this meant. One more person she was going to have to share her earnings with was all she could think of at the moment. Plugging her headset into the phone, she logged onto the computer as she spoke. "Everyone has a number they use. It's to keep track of their sales."

"Commissions." She nodded. Her eyes filled with tears when she thought of how much less her check was going to be now. "And do you keep track of them? Or does the company?"

"Both." *Fat lot of good it does me*, she thought. "Once you have your day finished, you'll want to print them up and...why are you really here? I mean, no one wants to be trained on how to do this job. It's just me."

"I don't understand." Nodding, she looked at the screen and tried her best not to cry. The tears were as useless as her aunt was. "Are you all right? Can I get someone for you?"

"It doesn't matter. Not at all." As she let out a long slow breath, she started training him. Telling him mostly what she did when she came in, how to log on, and anything else she could think of, especially how to clock in. "If you don't clock in, the computer won't compute your sales. All your work, if you do any, will be lost to you and put in an account somewhere. So it's really important that you clock into your computer and that no one else knows your sign on. They can really screw you over if they do."

"Who did it to you? Who is it that screwed you over?" She just stared at him when he repeated his questions. The man was entirely too nice.

Standing up, needing a few minutes, she picked up her chair—the collapsible one that she'd brought from home when her work one had been broken and not replaced—and bag and told him she'd be back. Nearly running to the bathroom, she found an empty stall and went in and locked the door.

It was too much. Her life had always been shitty, but this was really about as low as she could get. She had no money, even though she was working three jobs, no place to live. Very little clothing and no food.

Her car had blown up somewhere along the way, so far back now she didn't even remember where. She knew that at some point someone was going to realize it was hers and come looking for her. There had to be laws about abandoning dead cars. Her Aunt Jeanie had a nice place, thanks to her and some rich shit that was letting her stay there because she was old and in a wheelchair. Not that she needed it. Aunt Jeanie could get around as well as she could. But her aunt had decided that it made her look regal, and she liked the perks it gave her.

Laci couldn't even stay with her. Not that she couldn't, but her aunt thought that it would be better for Laci if she learned humility. Laci was pretty sure she couldn't get any more humiliated if she tried. But if she would buy her aunt's groceries, bring her milk, and also take out the trash, sweep and do a load or two of laundry, she would allow her to take a shower. Just as long as she didn't use her things and cleaned up after herself.

"Like I haven't done that my whole life." The door to the bathroom opened and she heard it close. Taking some toilet paper off the roll, she blew her nose and flushed the toilet. Coming out of the stall, she was surprised to see Blair there.

"What the hell are you doing?" She looked around the room, then back at him, not even bothering to answer. "There is a man at your desk that says you're training him. How did he get in here, and why are you of all people training him? I never gave you permission to do that. Nor did I hire him in the first place."

"He has an email." She went to the sink to wash her hands, then turned to look at him. "I only work here. You want to know why he's here, then I would suggest that you ask him."

The slap took her breath away. Staggering back from him, thinking he was going to hit her again had her afraid. When he stood there, his body stiff and hard, hands closing and opening, she felt the urge to run. Not just run but never stop once she got going.

"You're going to sit at that desk of yours and not do a damned thing with him until I get to the bottom of this. And if I find out you're lying, I'll take every penny of that commission check from you and burn it right in front of you. Do you hear me?" Nodding, she watched him. "You are nothing, do you hear me? Nothing unless I say so. If you think I'm going to put up with your bullshit, then you're stupider than the man who just bought this company. He thinks he's going to make changes. Well I have news for him. No one makes changes that I don't approve of. You hear me?"

"Yes." As he turned and left her, Laci looked in the mirror. His handprint was there, bright red against her skin. Taking one of the paper towels, she wet it and put it on her face. She asked herself the same question she did every time she looked in this particular mirror. "What the fuck are you doing here?"

Phillip was still at her desk, but Blair was with him. The man who had been in the bathroom resembled the one talking to Phillip in so many ways that she wondered if there were two of them. This version of Blair was polite, smiling, and looked nothing like the monster that had just hurt her. Pulling out her chair from its bag, she sat down on it and started to work. Whatever happened now, it was out of her hands.

"I was wondering about the chair thing and he said you were strange about things. I think someone is messing with you. Am I right? He also said you're the best, that I'd — Who hit you?" She jerked from his grip, but it did her little good. He pulled her back to look at her face, and she again felt the tears fill her eyes. "Who did this to you?"

"Just leave it alone. Please?" He just stared at her. Laci watched his face and knew when he'd figured it out. "Please? Just let it go. I only have two weeks left and I need this job until then."

"Why?" She turned to her computer when Phillip asked her the same question she'd been asking herself for three months now. "Is it because he wasn't aware I was coming? And he was pissed off?"

Shaking her head, mostly to dispel the notion that he sounded concerned, she started to tell him what he had to do to answer the phone. It was easier than telling him that her entire life for the last two years had been such a fuck up. And that she had not a single idea as to why.

"The head phones are to be on at all times. And remember whatever you say in them, even if you're not on a call, is being recorded." She pulled a notebook from her bag and handed him a pen as well. "I'm going to tell you things never to say to a customer. Don't tell them a lie. It will come back to bite you in the butt. Also, don't tell them to calm down. That'll make them madder in a heartbeat. Even though you have a script in front of you, don't sound as if you're reading from it. They know. And when they know, it will make them twice as mad as they were in the beginning."

He was writing things down as quickly as she told him. There were rules written down, several books of them that he could read, but there were things, too, that they never told you in them. Most of which she had learned on her own.

"What about turning someone's cable on or off? Can you do that?" She nodded, her mind drifting to the one time she'd turned someone's cable on without Blair's approval. And how much trouble she'd been in. "I know that there are men in the fields, but they aren't the only ones that can do that, are they?"

"Linemen. And mostly it's them. If there is a problem with a house, you have to put in a work order and then make a copy of it for your own file, as well as give a copy to Blair. He has final say over all that kind of stuff." Laci wondered why he did but had never cared to ask. "I understand there is a new owner. He might have a different way of doing things. You'll have to check with him."

A woman had had her cable shut off right after Laci had started working here. After doing some searching and pulling up other records, she'd found that the woman had unknowingly been paying her cable bill with an old account. The account had been closed when she'd moved, and no one had bothered to check why someone was paying with a dead account. Laci had been written up on a final warning for having the lineman go back to the house and turn her cable back on for her. She wasn't even sure that the money had ever been transferred to the new account, as she'd been blocked from the woman's account.

They answered about a dozen calls and Laci felt herself relax. When it was her break time, she told him where he could go and she picked up her things and put them in her bag. She'd learned not to leave things where anyone could get to them.

"Don't you have a chair?" She looked at the small collapsible chair in her hand, then at his nice comfy office chair. "I know there are more of these. Or do you just like this one?"

He was kind, that's what she decided to tell herself later, when she was regretting opening her mouth. Phillip had asked her, not demanded. It was the first bit of kindness she'd had in so long that she found herself wanting to tell him.

"They take it. And my things. I have no idea why. They make more money than.... I can't leave my things around. Not even things that are company owned. The last chair I had, the third one that I was issued, I had to pay for it when they cut into the cushion and broke the wheels off it. Pens too. I bring my own in because they sabotage the ones that are given to me. Ink gets on my clothing. They don't write. Or once, super glue was put on my pen while I was in the bathroom and I had to peel some of my flesh off to remove it from my fingers." Laci looked at the people she'd come to hate. "You should really just hang out with them. Whatever I teach you, you'll never use it. They've not made a single sale or call since I started working here."

"Have you reported them?" She laughed and felt her heart twist up. "Or is Blair in on it? Is that why he hit you?"

Laci knew she'd said too much. Gathering the last of her things, she told Phillip that he had about ten minutes before she'd be back. It was on the tip of her tongue to tell him to not come to her desk again, but she liked him. Even with them only just meeting, she felt as if she'd known him her entire life. But friendships could get her killed, and she decided to keep her mouth shut from now on. No matter how tempting it was to unload on him.

CHAPTER 2

Andrew was sitting at his new desk talking to Phillip through their link when Warren came in. Phillip was telling him everything that he'd learned and some things he had speculated about. Warren didn't knock but just barged in and sat in the chair across from. He wanted to get up and slap the shit out of the man. Instead, he smiled and asked him what he could do for him.

"There is a young man in my customer service department that claims that you hired him. I don't know why you'd do something like that when we both know that I'm going to have to let him go in a few days." Andrew asked him what he meant. "There are rules here. Ones that I have put into place so that there would be a good crew here. I don't care for you hiring anyone off the streets like this. From now on, when one of your buddies needs a job, send them to a place more suited to them. Perhaps the hamburger joint down the street."

"Oh? And even though this is my company, you feel that I should run my hiring through you?" Blair nodded and smiled at him. "I see. Anything else I should be passing by you first?"

"I'm so glad you asked. I would like to know first off, are you going to be showing up every day? I use this office at times, for meetings and such, and you have put me off my schedule with you being here all the time. Perhaps I can make you a schedule and you can come when it's not being used." Andrew was so shocked that he only nodded. "Also, the personnel files. I know that you've asked some of the staff to get them for you, and I wish you'd just stop doing that. I have them just the way I want them, and if you go mucking through them, there is no telling what you might do. I will tell you about each person working here if you wish to know. They're my family, after all."

"I see. And you know each person that works here." Blair told him again they were family. "What if I asked you about your customer service department? Even though as far as I know that department isn't under your job description, you'd be able to tell me all about the people working there."

"Of course. And everything is under my job description. I've been doing it for so long here that I know it better than anyone." He tisked at Andrew, and he felt the bubble of laughter come up to his throat. "We both know that you only purchased this place because it was a nice tax write-off for you. Rich men like you, in my experience, get bored easily, and you just buy things you don't need and then get bored with whatever bobble it was that you thought you'd change. There is no reason whatsoever for you to be here. I have things under control."

I need to talk to you. He asked Phillip to wait, he was talking to Warren. *Yeah, about him. He hit the girl I'm training with.*

Andrew felt his anger toward the man in front of him double, and he asked Phillip what had happened to her as Warren babbled on about the things he wanted Andrew to do from now on. Mostly to stay home and leave him alone. When Phillip told him what he thought was happening, as well as the rest of what he'd been telling him about the girl, he stood up. Warren did as well.

"Are you leaving? Oh good. I have two things I need to do on your computer. And then there is the—"

"I don't want you using my computer or this office again. I changed the password so that you can't anyway. And I'd very much like for you to give me the keys to these filing cabinets today. I want to look over all the records in them." Warren asked him why he'd do a fool thing like that. "Because it's my office and my computer, and most importantly, it's my fucking company. I'm having the locks changed today."

"Oh no, that won't work for me. I mean, unless you're planning to give me the keys. It will make it most difficult for me if you don't just give them to me when the man changes them out if you insist on wasting your money like that. I would hate to have to have someone come in and take the door off to get in if you don't cooperate with me." Andrew asked him why he'd do that when he'd just told him to stay out. "I told you. I used this office when I have meetings. What do you think would happen to this room if no one could get in? Why, it would be a waste of space. No, no. I think you should just leave things the way they are. And please don't lock out the computer. I have no time to be trying to figure out what you've used as a password. As I have said to you, I use that as well."

Andrew asked Phillip to call him. On the phone. Now. As soon as the phone rang, he told Warren that he needed to take this and to close the door on his way out. The man looked like he was going to argue, but Andrew turned his back to him. It was that or get up and knock the man on his ass. As soon as the door closed, Andrew turned back around and counted to ten. Phillip was laughing when he decided he was as calm as he was going to get right now. He told him what was going on with the other man.

"Yeah, he came down to the department I'm in and asked me what I thought I was doing there. When I showed him the email that you sent out, he then took off. When the girl returned, she was marked. He'd hit her and when I asked her about it, she cried." Andrew was going to get to the bottom of this shit now. "There's more. Do you want to hear it?"

"No. I don't think so. I just wanted to buy me a company, tear it apart, and put in something that I thought would be fun. I don't even watch cable." Phillip laughed. "This girl, it's like we thought it was, she's the one making the sales, isn't she? And they're taking them. I take it she's not doing this out of the kindness of her heart."

"Not hardly. And you might also like to know that she's on the run. I don't know who from because she doesn't." Andrew asked him if he'd taken a walk through her mind. "I have. There is a lot of pain in there too. She has an aunt that is a real piece of work. Oh, and by the way, she's living in one of Carter's places. The aunt, not the girl. Her name is Laci by the way. Laci Wintermute. There are some things I'm going to have Hannah look into for me. A shooting in Nevada. She was there, apparently, when things went south, and she hasn't a single idea why this person was after her."

"And this is the point where she started running?" Phillip said that he thought so. "Okay, let me look. And I need a favor. Can you hang out with her for a couple more days? This guy, there is something about him that makes me think that he's the one doing the sales changes, and that he's going to make Laci pay big time for today."

"I'd not doubt that at all. But no, I don't mind hanging out a couple more days. I feel really protective of her. And she's smart too. When I did my little walk, I found that she's homeless, so you know. Living in one of the buildings not far from here. I don't think she's safe there." Andrew said he'd have someone watch her. "Good. I was going to do it, but you can. Andrew, there is something incredibly sad about her. I don't mean like the kind that you've lost something and it's breaking your heart. But a deep sadness that makes me want to take her home with me and keep her safe. I don't think I've felt that way in a while."

Andrew called the locksmith and arranged for him to come out today. Then he called someone to come in and give his computer a look over, and to install some cameras in his office. Andrew had a feeling that a little thing like locks wouldn't keep Warren out of anywhere he felt he should be able to enter. Then he called Hannah. He told her what he had heard from Phillip and what he thought was going on.

"Yes. Here it is. Oh my." He asked her what she'd found. "Grocery store robbery gone bad. Six dead, including the store manager and a cop. Wait, not a cop, but a man dressed as one. They're still trying to figure out why he was there."

"Do they have any leads?" She said that it didn't appear so. "Any mention of a woman by the name of Wintermute?"

"No. But hang on." While he listened to the keys on her computer click, he looked at his computer's history. There were things on it that he knew he'd never looked at. Before he could look into things, Hannah spoke again. "Wintermute is mentioned in another article. Several as a matter of fact. A Laci shows up several times in the college happenings, a local college paper as being in the dean's list...let me see. Fourteen times. Impressive. Full time student. Fluent in several languages. Then there is an obit. Only child of Peter and Sarah Wintermute. An aunt too. Jeanie Wintermute is mentioned. That was four years ago. Doesn't say what happened."

"Phillip said that it's the girl that I was telling you about from the cable company." She asked him if it was the one giving up her sales. "Yes. But I don't think it's so much she's giving them up as they're being taken from her. I think this piece of shit here is making her somehow. And she goes by Beth Summer."

"Her middle name is Elizabeth. And Wintermute? Probably why she goes by Summer." He nodded and realized that she couldn't see him, and told her he thought she might be right. "I have to go to the doctor's in an hour. Max is gone with Kendra, so I'm coming in alone. Wanna take me to lunch and let me swing by and meet this girl?"

"I'd love to have lunch with you. But Phillip is going to be with her a couple more days until I get this figured out, and I will." She told him she knew he would. "Where are Kendra and Max this week?"

Kendra, the queen of the Genjar that his other sister-in-law was a part of, had decided that she needed some downtime. Last week she and Max had gone to an amusement park for the entire week, riding rides and eating junk food. The two of them were accompanied by the royal guard so no one was worried that they'd get hurt, but Andrew was slightly jealous of the two of them. The two of them were having a blast last he'd heard from them.

"Hiking. And before you claim that sounds tame or something like that, they're hiking in the Smoky Mountains. Backpacking it across the entire park and taking pictures, Max told his mom. Murph said that they're living off the land and sleeping in a tent. She was pretty sure that they're both loving every minute of it." Hannah laughed, then moaned. "This little guy is really getting huge, and I don't know how much longer I can go with him in there."

"You've only got a few days left. You feeling okay?" Hannah, was married to Misha—his oldest brother—and was pregnant. So were some of his other sisters-in-law. Linyah, who was married to his brother Thomas, was due in three months. His other sister-in-law, Murph—who was married to Carter—was due in five. While Phillip and Charlie weren't having a baby just yet, he knew that they would be soon. Their mom was in heaven, knitting every day and keeping the nursery full of booties and blankets. "You'd think Mom would be thrilled with having a baby in the house soon and leave Rider and me alone. But I think she's harder on us now to find a mate than she'd been before."

"She just wants to see you guys as happy as we are. And we are." Andrew laughed. "Are you ready for your mate, Andrew? I mean, if she comes along now, are you going to shove her away?"

"No. I don't know what I'd do, but I know that I'd be open-minded and open-hearted. I've seen the way my brothers have gone about this, mucking things up. I don't want that to happen with me." He thought of Misha and how he'd done Hannah when he'd first met her. "Besides, I have you and the rest of the women in my family to knock me around a bit should I fuck up."

"You know I will too." When someone knocked on his door, he told them to come in. Hannah laughed again. "I should get going myself. I know you're busy. I'll look into this some more and come by to pick you up for lunch. Okay?"

"I'd love nothing better." He told her he'd see her and hung up and looked at John Wentworth, his expert computer guy, with Blair right behind him. Andrew stood up and moved to the door. Blair was opening his mouth to no doubt tell him he wasn't going to do this when Andrew told him to get out.

"I've explained to you why you can't do this. Whatever am I going to do if you come in here changing things? Do you have any idea how much longer it's going to take me to do my job if I have to keep working around your mess?" Andrew only backed him out the door. "Mr. Lanning, you're making things very difficult for me. And I just don't like it. You're not cooperating with me and you're going to have to do as I want soon or I'll just have to write you up."

"Yeah, you go ahead and try that on me. But so you know, I don't care." Slamming the door in Blair's face when he was out of his office, Andrew stood there trying to control his cat and his temper. The fucker was going to make him hurt him if he kept this up.

"I'm assuming that you want the works." Andrew turned and looked at John when he spoke. "He's a little shit, but I'm thinking you figured that out already."

"He doesn't want me to change my computer because he claims that he needs it more than I do." John laughed and sat down at the computer desk. "What do you see when you look at this?"

"Cloned." Andrew knew what he meant but asked him to explain to be sure. "Your computer has a cloning program on it. I would say that the little fucker has done it. Whatever you touch, he can see. History, files. Even emails. He can get into them."

"You only just sat down. How the hell did you know that?" John laughed and pressed on a few keys, then showed him the running program. He also showed him where the camera on his desktop was running. "He can see me in here?"

"Yeah, pretty much. Conversations too. And to be honest with you, I saw it on his computer out there. I only glanced at it, but it was the same as you have here." Andrew asked him if he could disable it. "I can, but if I were you, I'd start fresh. If he can do this, which I'm assuming he did, there might be more programs running that I haven't found yet. I'd also disable the camera on a new one too. You having someone setting some up in here?"

"Yes. I told Darin to say he was going to open the files behind you. And to change the locks on the doors. I explained to him that the fucker, an apt name for him by the way, was going to ask him about ten thousand questions and try to send him away." As John worked at his desk, pulling out the old computer and getting things boxed up, Andrew thought of the girl again. Pulling out his phone, he started doing some digging on his own.

~~~

Phillip was doing a great job. He'd been using her phone and computer for the last hour and he was making great headway in getting the job down pat. When they had a break again, he asked her to come outside with him, that he needed some fresh air.

"I have to tell you something." She nodded and sat down. "I like you, Beth, I really do. But I've been less than honest with you. I'm not just a new hire. And my name isn't Phillip. Well, it is, but it's really my first name and not my last. My brother, Andrew, he's the new owner of the company."

She thought of some of the things she'd said to him and stood up to run. He asked her to stay, that he wanted to talk to her. *Yeah*, she thought, *this will be the end of my workday right here*. Even though she was going to quit anyway, she had a feeling that she'd not see Friday's check now.

"You were spying on me." He shook his head, then nodded. "Yeah, well, in the event you didn't get that, that wasn't the least bit helpful. Were you or were you not sent to spy on me? It was Blair, right? He said some things to your brother and you came in to...I don't know. You came in to see if any of it's true. Well, it's not."

"No, it's not. And that's not why I'm here. I came to see why anyone would be giving away hundreds of dollars of their sales commissions like you were doing." Laci said nothing but did sit down again. "Andrew, my brother, bought this company to break it down. There's no need for this little company, and he simply wanted something to do. He and I are actually opening an antique hardware store with our brother...never mind. That's not important. But he saw the way your sales were being disturbed, and he sent me here to find out why."

"You could have asked me." He asked her if she would have told him. "No. I can't. But you could have just asked."

She got up to pace, wishing now that she'd remembered to get a bottle of water to go with her crackers. Laci felt the tears threaten again and decided that she'd had enough of being a doormat to men. When she turned to look at him again, she saw something...something moved over him, and she took a step back.

"Don't. If you run, I'm going to not be able to hold onto him." She asked him who. "I'm not human."

"Not human." He nodded. "As in you're something else. Like a monster or something. And so you know, right now, I think you are, a monster I mean. What you did to me is beyond cruel. I trusted you."

"That's why I wanted to talk to you." She nodded but said nothing else. All she could really think of was he'd said he wasn't human. "I'm a cat. Leopard as a matter of fact."

"I don't believe you." He put out his arm, and she turned her back on him. "I don't want you to...I said I didn't believe you. Not that I don't think you're telling me the truth. I just want you to go away."

"I can't do that. I feel an overwhelming need to protect you." She nodded, her back still to him. "I know you're on the run. I also know that your name is Laci Wintermute. You have an aunt that lives in one of the apartments over on Ninth. Which another brother of mine owns."

She turned and looked at him. "You investigated me? How the hell...? How the hell did you find out my name? I've been very careful with that. Did you read my mind?" Phillip nodded. "No. I mean no. You can't do that. People can't really read other people's mind."

"I can. I know everything there is to know about you. Where you're living, how much money you have, and where you have it stashed. I know that you lost your parents several years ago to a car accident and that you've been taking care of your—" She told him to stop. "I'm sorry, Laci. I really am. But I want to help you."

"No. I mean hell no. I don't want your help." She started pacing again and tried to think. "I don't know how you did this. Nor do I like that you're spying on me. You know that there are people chasing me? And do you know why? Are you a part of it? Is that it?"

"No. I don't know who they are or what they want because you don't. If Max were here, he'd more than likely know." She asked him who that was. "My nephew. He's the son of my brother's wife. Murph...Dane Murphy Lanning."

"The sheriff? You're related to the sheriff of this little town? Well of course you are. Why the fuck not?" When he nodded, Laci felt the earth shift under her feet when she got dizzy. When he helped lower her to the ground, she stayed where she was. This was just too much. "Your brother now owns the company that I work for. Another brother owns the place that my aunt is living in. The sheriff is your sister-in-law, and you're not human. Can this break get any more surreal?"

"Yes." He got down to her level and said her name. "My brother Thomas is married to a princess and she's a genjar. Murph is Doran, as is her son, and I guess my brother is now. And my wife, Charlie, can do some pretty freaky shit too."

"You're not helping." He laughed and she smiled at him. "Is any of this true? I mean, one thing of it? I'll be okay that you only said it to try and cheer me up."

Instead of answering her, he put his hand on her outstretched leg and it changed. Fur sort of just consumed his arm, and long claws appeared at the tips of his fingers. When she looked at his face, she could see that cat there too. His eyes were darker, his face looked fuller, longer. And when he shook his body, like he was shaking rain off his head, he was Phillip again.

"All the rest is true as well." Nodding, she sat there. It was too much if she was honest with herself. Mind overload, and she couldn't think beyond just making her body work, breathing in and out, and trying to keep from running and screaming. "Are you all right?"

"My break is over." She stood up then and moved toward the building. If he followed her, she really didn't care. Function, her mind told her, just function. But just as she was walking into the door, something hit her and knocked her back on her ass. The pain in her head exploded just as she saw what she'd hit.

A man...no, that was too tame a word. A god had hit her. A god that worked in her building? Who knew? But nothing would surprise her much right now.

CHAPTER 3

Andrew sat as still as he could and watched the two doors that led to the rooms in the emergency room. He had been counting the strokes that the second hand made when he'd been told to sit and shut up, but that wasn't working any more to keep him or his cat calm. He had to...no, he really needed to go and see the woman again. Looking at his brother Phillip, he wondered if he'd help him clear this up, and decided that he didn't know if he could say the words out loud. Phillip spoke before he could find out if he would or not.

"I think you pissed that doctor and nurse off." He nodded. Andrew knew that. And Phillip had saved him from being arrested. Murph came in a few minutes later when he'd been surrounded by security to be thrown out of the hospital and told him in no uncertain terms to sit here and not move. "I don't think Murph is all that happy with you either."

"I think she's my mate. That woman you were working with, I think she's my mate." Phillip looked at him and Andrew could tell he thought he was joking. "My cat wants to go back there and tear everyone apart so he can touch her, and I'm not so calm either."

Phillip stoop up and told him to come with him. Andrew stayed where he was. Not because he was afraid of Murph. She had threatened to castrate him, but he wasn't sure he wanted to know.

"You can't tell from here. And as much as I'd like to just see your cat go ape shit about now, I don't think Murph will hesitate in shooting your ass." He nodded, still not moving. "Why aren't you sure? The blood throw you off?"

"No. I was...I was pissed off. I mean really pissed off, and I think it clouded my judgment." Phillip asked him if he really believed that. "Yes. I mean no. I don't fucking know."

"Well, you'd better figure this out soon. Mom and Misha are on their way in, and they're not all that thrilled with this either." He asked him why. "Because that little shit you hit before leaving your office is suing you."

"He hit me first." Phillip only cocked a brow at him. "Okay, I guess I could have pulled back a little, but he actually hit me. And told me that I needed to go home and take a nap. I'm a grown fucking man."

"Well, then act like it." Andrew closed his eyes at the sound of his mom's voice behind him. When he stood up and turned to look at her, Misha and Hannah were right behind her. "And I would appreciate it if you were to curb that tongue of yours as well. Whatever were you thinking, Andrew Lanning? Or were you?"

"He thinks she's his mate." Andrew wanted to hit his brother but knew if he drew back, it would be a brutal war. "He was just going back to find out now. And that guy? The one he hit? He hit her before Andrew hit him. I think that he deserved that and more for hitting her in the first place."

"Well, shit." His mom turned and looked at Misha when he spoke. "I'm sorry, Mom, but this guy hit one of our females. I don't know about you, but I think that justifies what he did."

"Be that as it may. In the future, please try not to break a man's jaw or his nose until you're sure." She took his arm and led him to the desk. "Andrew, who is this young lady?"

"I have no idea." She looked at him oddly, but then spoke to the nurse at the desk. In seconds he was headed back to the emergency department with his mom and the nurse. This wasn't going to go well, he knew it.

The nurse coming out of the curtained-off area looked nervous. When she saw the person that was with them, she came toward them as if she was glad to have someone else there. Andrew walked to the curtained area and threw back the curtain back. Not only was the messy bed empty, but the cubical looked empty as well. He turned to the two nurses.

"Where is she?" They looked at each other, then at him. "She ran, didn't she? I mean, unless you have her hidden in your pocket, she's left without your consent."

"She said that she had no insurance. And even if she could have afforded it, there wasn't any way for her to pay for the deductible." Andrew was nodding as he reached for his brothers to tell them what was going on. The nurse continued. "Poor little thing. When she woke up, she was so terrified that it took me nearly ten minutes to get her to calm down. But I did manage to give her something for pain."

"What did you give her?" When Andrew heard what it was, he revised his message to his brothers. *She might be out of it by the time you find her. They gave her a nice dose of drugs to help her out, so maybe she's close by and we won't have to look too long to get her back here. I have no idea where to even begin. Try the buildings Phillip was talking about that she might be in.*

43

Andrew left the hospital to search for Laci after assuring his mom that he was going to be careful with her whether she was his mate or not. Talking with Phillip, he gained a great deal of personal information including her name, but he was still at a loss as to whether or not she was actually his mate.

Just as he was leaving the building, he saw Thomas. As they came together in the parking lot, Andrew had the most insane need to hug him. He explained everything that had happened so far, as well as who the girl might be to him. That was when Thomas told him he knew where the girl was.

"She's not having an easy time of it. And when I did a search of the area for her like I was asked, I found a woman a few blocks from here that was in a great deal of pain. It's receding now with the drugs I guess, but we have to find her. It's why I came here as quickly as I could. You're not going to like this, but I also have an idea who might want her dead." Andrew stopped walking and looked at Thomas. "Sonya. I mean, I'm not positive, but I think it might be her. Sina said that she would have set it up so that none of us meet our mates, and that since you think this girl is yours, it would stand to reason that she'd be a target."

They drove to the building and were parking when he saw Laci. She was leaning against the wall to the smallest of the three abandoned buildings and there were two men with her. He could see that she was having some difficulties and got out of the car just as Thomas said his name.

"If you kill them, there will be hell to pay. Not just from the police, but Mom will rip you a new ass." Andrew knew that too but asked him what he was to do. "Just go there, get her, and come back here. Don't engage in a war play with those idiots. They're not worth it."

"It might be to me." Thomas just rolled his eyes. "All right. I'll try to behave. But I'm not making any promises. I've had a really shitty day so far."

"I would say that she has too. Don't you think?" That calmed him and his cat just a little. "Go easy. As you know, Phillip has talked to her and she seemed all right with what he said, but she might still freak out a little."

Phillip had told him what he'd shown her as well as the things he'd told her. She had needed something, he'd told him, to get her mind off of the fact that she had been robbed by his company. He also told him that he had to protect her. And now that they knew she was his mate, that explained a great deal.

The men with her were touching her, not hurting her that he could see, but they were trying to get her to go with them. Andrew politely but firmly told them to back off. The first guy did as he asked, the second one simply cupped her breast.

"Don't do that." The man, the soon to be dead man, laughed. "I really don't want to have to explain to my sister-in-law, the sheriff, why I had to kill you. I mean, she's already pissed off at me for punching a man in the face and breaking his jaw and his nose. I'm pretty sure that he might need surgery too. He's kind of disfigured from when I hit him in the face with a bat too. I don't know for sure. But if you don't back away from my wife, I'm going to kill you."

"She's not your wife. If she was, where did her ring go?" Andrew reached into the man's head and made him back off. He neither had the time for this nor did he want to have to hit him. As soon as she was let go, Laci fell forward and he caught her in his arms.

"You did that really well and no one had to die. See, you can be taught how to be nice." Andrew snorted at Thomas as he got into the car with Laci. Lifting her throat to his nose, he inhaled deeply. It was her. This woman was his mate and he told Thomas, who laughed. "Now what?"

"I have no idea. I guess the hospital. Or Mom's. Which do you think?" Thomas told him hospital even as he was starting his car. "She's not going to be too terribly happy about this, is she?"

"I don't think I would be if I were her."

As they drove along, Andrew looked at her. He wanted to touch the large bump on her head but didn't. He wanted her to be quiet for a few more minutes, and he was afraid if he touched her right now, he might hurt her. Pulling up in front of the hospital, he saw not just his mom but the rest of his family as well. This was going to be bad, he knew it.

~~~

Laci felt the warm blankets over her body and snuggled down under them. She couldn't remember the last time she'd been warm in her bed. Nor, for that matter, the last time her bed had been so nice. She opened her eyes when she realized she'd not even had a bed in a few months, yet here she was in one. The man sitting in front of her was staring at her.

He was leaning forward, his arms on his knees, and looked ready to pounce, like a cat did when it saw a mouse. Laci watched him, thinking that was the strangest thought she'd ever had about a stranger before. Then she remembered Phillip and his arm.

"My name is Andrew Lanning." She nodded and felt the sharp pain in her head. "You have ten stitches in the back of your head from the fall. The bump on your forehead is getting better but still will be painful for a few more days. Or so they told me when I asked."

"Who are *they*?" He answered her, still not moving from his position in the chair. "I left the hospital in favor of not having to pay for a huge bill that I can't afford. How did I get back here?"

"I brought you. I had to find you first, which proved to be an adventure. There were two men with you that had decided that you might have been a tasty treat for them." Laci wondered if he was frozen or something. He hadn't moved so much as his finger since she'd been looking at him. "Do you hurt?"

"I do. I'm pretty sure that's about par for the course when you have stitches in your head and are in the hospital. But that doesn't negate the fact that I'm not able to afford this." He didn't say anything, and she thought that she'd gladly hit him. "What are you doing here? I mean, have you nothing better to do than to sit in a chair staring at a stranger?"

"You work for me." That did nothing to dispel her wondering why he was here. "And I hit you. I mean, I knocked you back when you came in the door. It's my fault that you're here."

"You mean the cable company…that's the job where I work for you? Or is it worked for you, as in I've been fired?" He shook his head. "I gave my notice there. I guess it's safe to assume you know that."

"No. I had no idea. That guy, Warren, he has the files and I had only just got the drawers open when I hit him. I think I pissed him off when I wanted to see the files on the people who worked for me. He seems to think I should just stay home. And take a nap. He said I needed to go home and take a nap. So I hit him." She asked him why he'd done that. "Because he's an arrogant ass that needed it long before I did it. Do you need me to get you anything for pain?"

"Are you a doctor as well as a cable mogul?" He said no. "Then I doubt very much you can help my pain. Besides, I'm pretty sure they'll want like fifty dollars a pill, and I can't afford that any more than I can this stay."

"I'm paying for it." She cocked a brow at him. "It's the least I can do after what we did to you. You know my brother, Phillip? I talked to him earlier too. He said he talked to you about what we are."

"You mean that shifting thing." He smiled then, and Laci felt like the sun had shone all over her body. "Don't do that. It's unfair."

"Do what?" She told him. "So you don't want me to smile because it warms you up? I'm betting I can warm you more if you'd let me."

He moved. Not just moved but was suddenly there, standing next to her. Laci rolled to her back and looked up at him. Christ, he was tall. Gorgeous and very tall. When he curled his fingers into hers, the warmth of his grip made her body heat and her nipples tighten.

He leaned down, his body almost in half when he brushed his mouth over hers. It was hot. His breath seemed to burn over her mouth. When he touched his mouth to hers, firmly this time, Laci moaned. There was no way this guy was only just kissing her. It felt like he was consuming her. And when he lifted his head, she looked into his blue eyes and thought she saw something there. Something that moved.

"Can I kiss you again?" His voice was low but dangerously sexy. Before she could figure out how to make her mouth work again, her head was nodding. This time when he touched his mouth to hers, Laci knew she was in deep shit.

The kiss, such a tame word for something that she felt running in her bloodstream, was hungry. He seemed to not just be kissing her, his tongue ruling hers as if he owned it, but that he was laying claim. And when he pulled her closer to him, nearly pulling her from the bed, Laci felt as if she had no choice but to wrap her arms around him and to hold on. It was that or she was sure she was going to fly away. When he lifted his mouth from hers, she whimpered.

"I need you." She found that she needed him as well and nodded. "But this is neither the time nor the place for me to lay you out on this bed and have my way with every inch of you."

"Why not?" Even as the words left her mouth, she felt her temper rise. "I don't...please put me back. And step away. I don't know what sort of drugs they gave me, but I don't talk like that. And I certainly don't beg men to take me. Please, put me down."

He only held her, and before she could try and be sterner with him, if she even thought she could, he kissed her again. This time she had no doubt that he needed her when he laid over her after laying her back on the bed. His hands too, were making short work of her gown.

His cock was hard, hitting her between her legs in the perfect place to make her wet and warm. When he rocked down, his entire body pressing into hers, Laci grabbed his shoulders again. This time she wasn't just hanging on, but she felt that if she didn't touch him now, she was going to die. Naked flesh filled her hands. His muscles seemed to ripple along her skin as he continued to torment her body. And when he suckled her breast into his mouth, tugging hard on her nipple, Laci cried out. Christ, she could come like this.

"I want to taste you." She wanted to point out that he had been until he stopped, but he grinned at her and she wanted to whimper again. "I want to eat you, Laci. Will you come for me while I do? Let me taste your creaminess as it fills me?"

"Please? I don't know why, but I need to come. Hurry." He moved down her body, stripping off what was left of her gown. When he was at her navel, his mouth sucked the small indentation and she held him there with her fingers curled into his soft hair. If he ate her pussy like he was her belly, she was going to come hard enough to blow the top off her head and the building she was in.

When he stood up, she watched him as he unbuttoned his shirt and tossed it on the chair behind him. She wondered if he could feel her need as she was his. Could he smell her like she thought for sure she was him? His musky odor, his body heat. It was all she could do not to beg him to let her have a bite of him. Then he pulled his belt off and dropped it on the floor.

"Are you going to have sex with me?" Her voice was hardly recognizable to her own ears. He nodded and she felt her pussy heat, her nipples tighten even more. When his nostrils flared, his head lifting to smell deeper, she spread her legs for him, the need to have him know that she wanted him as badly making her reckless. "I need you. I have no idea why...this is insane, but I can't stop myself from wanting to feel your mouth on me. Your cock deep inside of me."

"You're mine." It sounded perfect to her, to be owned by a man, this man. And when he opened his fly, she could see the tip of his cock, the dark crown there, and licked her lips. "I'm going to eat you until you scream. Then I'm going to pull you off that bed and fuck you hard enough that you know how much I need you."

"Yes. Please. I need you." He pulled her legs to the side of the bed. She felt strange, her legs wide, her body spread before him, but when he pulled the chair to the bed, the one he'd been sitting in, she watched as he sat down in it and rolled it to her. Laci felt her pussy soak again and nearly closed her legs, she was so embarrassed at what he could see now.

"Open them for me, Laci. I want to watch you come. I want to see your cream flow from you while you do it." She watched him lower his head, his mouth poised to take her when he spread her nether lips open. The coolness after being so hot and wet made her moan. "Come for me. While I watch, come."

He only touched her. His finger or thumb just brushed over her clit and his hot breath sent her over the edge. Laci came hard, her body seemingly on the brink of it since she'd woken up. And when he sucked her clit into his mouth and nipped at her, Laci came a second time, bringing her body up off the bed when she did.

He ate her. Devoured her to the point where she wasn't sure she could take much more. Every time she came, and there were just too many times to count, she felt as if it wasn't enough and too much at the same time. And that, while satisfying, she knew there was more to come. Something powerful and mind blowing. When he stood up, his cock thick and bare to her, she wanted to take him into her mouth and drink him down, have the cream at his tip slide down her throat like he had her.

"I can't wait." She nodded, reaching for him even as he rubbed his crown over her clit until she came twice more. "Christ, I need you."

He slammed into her. There wasn't any kind of sliding gently into her pussy. He powered into her. His body became as much a part of her as her hand or arm. She came around him, feeling as if he'd woken something in her that only he could have done. She held him to her, screaming out her release even as a second one took her under. And when he lifted her legs up to get deeper, closer to her, Laci wrapped her legs around him and reached for him. As soon as his mouth covered her breast again, she dug her nails into his back. Need was spiraling out of control, but she was almost afraid to let go, to let the release that was just there, on the edge, come over her.

His mouth was everywhere. Every time he touched her at her breast or neck, she wanted to give him more. His hands followed his mouth, squeezing and cupping parts of her that until this very moment she'd never thought of as sensual. And when his mouth was at her throat, right over her pounding pulse, she felt her body tense. Whatever he was going to do to her now, it was going to take her away.

"Come for me."

She felt it come over her. Not like a gentle rain, but a finger in a socket kind of feeling. And when he bit her, tearing at her throat, she felt her entire being stop. Her heartbeat stopped pumping blood to her body, her mind froze like she'd been eating ice cream too fast. Even her skin seemed to know that something was coming. In that moment Laci had a clarity about this that she knew was epic. Laci fell in love with the man fucking her. And then she not only fell over the edge of a very high cliff, but went over it willingly as she came again and again.

He brought her twice more. Each time she felt as if she were giving him more of her, her heart, her body and everything that made her who she was. And when he came too, every part of her body felt it. He branded her, marked her in a way that made her realize that she'd never be the same again.

"Come," he commanded of her again. As his body filled hers with his cum, she screamed. The energy of her release needed to be expelled and the scream was just the beginning of it. Laci needed more, needed it all, and when he held her to his throat, she bit down on his throat hard enough to taste blood.

As it filled her mouth, then slid down the back of her throat, she cried out again as she drank greedily from the wound she'd created. Laci felt herself falling down a long tunnel, darkening as she went until there was simply nothing.

CHAPTER 4

Andrew dressed but kept an eye on Laci. He'd covered her with the sheet that had ended up on the floor, but he felt like she was still exposed to everyone. The nurse that had come in to take her blood pressure had only looked at the room, then at him, before going out and returning with a clean gown as well as two blankets. While she did her job, Andrew tried to think what he needed to do now.

He'd mated. And every time he thought of that, the sappy feeling would settle over him and he'd have to drag his thoughts back to what he had to do now. And he was pretty sure there was plenty. Like where the hell were they going to live? He had a place to stay but nothing in it. Not even a couch or a decent bed. Andrew looked at Max when he suddenly appeared in the room with him and Kendra standing just to his right.

"We wanted to see how you're doing." He nodded but said nothing. Kendra moved to the bed while Max, Murph's son, stood near him and continued. "She'll work for me. In my business, all right?"

"She has a job." He shook his head at him. "She works for the cable company. The one I just bought."

"It's no longer safe for her there. Blair Warren will make it more difficult for her than he had before. And someone is coming for her." Andrew glanced at Kendra and then back at Max. "Thomas is correct. It is Sonya's men. They don't care that their master is dead. They have a job to do and nothing will keep them from it. I know that there is something for them if they succeed, but I don't have any idea what it might be right now."

"Why? Is it because of her idea that we weren't to have mates?" Max said that was it, but Andrew had a feeling it was more than that. "I can't keep her safe if she's not where I can see her all the time."

"If they kill her, her death, if they find her there, will be the end of you and you know it." Kendra sat down on a nice chair that hadn't been there before as she spoke to him. "In the building where she'd be working for Max, it will be safer for her. There are elements that she can use there that will make it so no one can enter if they have ill will in their heart. Much like you have at the homes where you live. While she is only a human, Max and I have put magic in place that will keep her as safe as if you're with her."

"Why?" Kendra asked him what he meant. "Why are you doing this for her? I mean, like you said, she's my mate, and since I'm sure you know that I've claimed her, she's the same as I am. Immortal, and can heal a great deal faster than a normal human can. Why are you taking precautions to keep her safer? Or is she not really a human but something else that has been hidden away until now?"

"No, she's only a human. Or was until you bonded with her. And yes, she's like you now, an immortal. But as for keeping her safe.... What if I told you that I know she holds the key? And that I don't know what the key unlocks or what is inside of whatever it is she's to open?" He told her he

56

didn't believe her. "Be that as it may, it's the truth. I know that she has the key. I haven't any idea if it's metaphysical or just key. But she has it. She's also the glue that holds the rest of you together when things go badly."

"What's going to happen?" Again, she told him she didn't know. "I thought you were all knowing and all powerful. How can things slip by you without you knowing about it?"

"I am all powerful but not all-knowing." Kendra looked at Laci, then back at him as she continued. "Laci is mentioned in the notes from Sonya that we've found. Most of it just talks about how she's a human, pretty easily disposed of. But over the years, not only did Sonya seem to have trouble getting her to die, she also seemed to get madder and madder with each thing that didn't work. And from the notes, Sonya tried everything."

"Her parents." Kendra nodded but said nothing more. "I had someone investigate her. I found that her parents were in a horrific accident about four years ago, and both of them were killed instantly. You're saying that Sonya was responsible for their deaths?"

"Yes. And many more that Laci had contact with. Her great aunt, her grandfather's sister, is the only one that has never had any harm come to her. I've been looking into that as well." Andrew knew about the aunt and what she had been doing to Laci since she'd resumed care for her after her father's death. "I've taken some liberties as well. With your home."

"Home? I don't have a home. And what sort of liberties have you taken in a home that I don't have? And why?" Kendra said nothing but stood up and faced the bed. Andrew did as well. "Kendra, are you talking about my apartment? If so, then you should know that I'm planning to find us a house."

"You have a home now. The apartment that you were living in won't be as safe. Hush now, she's waking up." Kendra turned to him. "We must go. Max and I are having tubes of meat on a stick over an open fire tonight. I know that they're hot dogs, but I so love the look on people's faces when I say that."

Then she was gone. He looked over at Max and wondered not for the first time just how powerful the boy was. It was scary what he could do. When he got up and touched his finger to Laci's bare arm, he disappeared too. Andrew decided that he simply wasn't going to ask.

He could tell Laci was embarrassed the moment she looked up at him, or tried not to look at him. Andrew was okay with that for now. What they had done had been amazing, wonderful, and consuming for him as well. When she pulled her hand from his when he took it in his, he took it back and kissed the back of it.

"Are you mad at me or just afraid?" Her flare of temper nearly made him laugh, but he wisely caught himself. While she didn't yell or scream at him, he could see that she did want to hit him. "I have never in my life enjoyed sex that much. I mean, I feel like you blew my head off and put it back on several times."

"I did no such thing. You know it was simply sex. I mean, it was fucking fantastic sex, but that's all it was." He sat down on the edge of the bed and continued to hold her hand. "We shouldn't have done that. You must know that as well. We're strangers. I mean, you know nothing at all about me and I don't you either."

"True. Very true. But that doesn't mean that I wouldn't like to strip you down and have my way with every inch of you again and again." Her face reddened and he smiled at her. "I actually know a great deal about you. I mean, I had you investigated. Before we made love."

"You did not." He nodded at her and watched her face. Her anger was there, as well as a deep seeded need to run. Andrew wanted to reassure her, tell her he was going to keep her safe, but he needed her to trust him. Now more than ever. "There are people after me. I don't suppose in your investigation you figured out what they want, did you? And don't think I'm okay with you having me looked into either. You had no right."

"You worked for me. And while I was trying to figure out what to do with my company, I saw your name. At least the name you were going by there. But I'll get to that in a moment." She still wasn't looking at him, and he reached down and lifted her chin up so that she was. "Are you upset with what we did? I mean, mad at me over it?"

"It wasn't as if I just laid there and let you do those things to me. I rather enjoyed it myself. But it was wrong. On so many levels." He didn't bother telling her that to him it wasn't, because he didn't think she'd appreciate that much honesty right now. "Why did my name stick out to you? I mean, there are over a hundred people working there. What made me so special?"

"Besides just being you? Your sales reports." Her body stiffened, and he felt her try and pull from his hand again. "Don't leave me. I need to talk to you about things. Not just on a personal level, but about work too. I need you to tell me why Warren hit you."

"He's a prick." He laughed and told her he agreed. "He was angry that I'd been training Phillip. He said he was your brother. Phillip I mean, he told me you were his brother. And that...and that you were...." She looked at his arm, then back at his face. "Blair has it in his head that he owns me and that cable company. He rules with an iron hand. And him hitting me was just the end of a long line of shit he's done to me. Mainly my commissions."

"Phillip told you that we're cats. And yes, Warren does think he owns the company, but I assure you that he's going to be gone soon. But to my brothers. Phillip is my younger brother. I have four more at home, all older than Phillip and I." Andrew turned his hand over so that his was on top. He let just a little of his cat go and she did jerk from him then. But before he could pull his cat back, she put her shaking hand over his furred one. "He wants to mark you as I have done. Not with sex, but with his tongue and bite."

"I bit you." The shocked look on her face had him thinking all sorts of thoughts, but she continued before he could tell what she was thinking about. "I had to. I mean, not just that it was fun because you bit me, but I really needed to sink my teeth into you and taste your blood. That's just not normal, you know that, don't you?"

"You had to because I'm your mate. We're a couple. And now that we've had sex and exchanged blood, we're inseparable." He knew she was going to argue with him. Andrew could see it in her eyes. "I promise you, we'll talk about this later. I really need to talk to you about Warren. He's pissed off at me, and I need to have a little talk with him."

"You mean about my commissions." He said it was more than that, but that was a good start. "I have all my sales reports. Or at least I did. I left them...I guess they're still at the company. When I got hurt I didn't get my things."

"Phillip got them for you. And the things that were on the desk. I had no idea when I took this company that you were going to be there, I wanted you to know that." She nodded. "When did he start moving your money around? And did you ever talk to him about it?"

"I did." She told him about the meeting that they'd had and that he'd told her that he had rules she had to follow. "The more I made, the more he'd take. I was making what amounted to a base pay. He'd make sure that I had just enough, or in this case not enough to be able to afford anything, including a place to stay. And he wasn't going to stop. He came right out and told me if I slowed my sales, he'd go to the police. At this point, I really don't care. So I applied for another job that would work around my other two jobs and gave my notice. I slipped the letter under your door when I found out that there was a new owner."

"I never saw it. And I'm pretty sure I know why not now. Warren has been going in and out of my offices since I bought the place. Even before that, he told me. Mostly he just rearranges my stuff to suit his needs. I wasn't aware of that then. I kept thinking the place was haunted and that the ghost was having fun with me." When she didn't find his lame joke funny, he moved on. "Then yesterday morning I called in some help. I had the locks changed and the computer removed and replaced. He'd cloned it."

"He had one on the computer I was using too. And he'd listen in on my sales pitches. I think that's the way he gets around certain things. Like when someone is leaving or looking for another position in the company, he spies on them to get them fired. I'm not a model employee, but I do make it so these people in his click are well paid." Andrew could see that. Keeping her around was better than having no extra cash for him. "He's going to be pissed off when he figures out what you've done to him."

"He already has found out. He and I had words the day I hurt you. I had just broken his jaw and nose and was pissed off and not paying attention to where I was going." She laughed and he did as well. Andrew loved the sound, feeling her good humor all the way to his toes. "You do know that what he's doing to you, it's not just illegal but it's also against any kind of company policy ever written. He's going to serve some major jail time when this comes out."

"He won't. It's been my experience that people like him get away with nearly murder, and no one seems to give a shit so long as it doesn't involve them." Andrew told her that he didn't work that way. "I'd watch my back then. He's a sneaky bastard and will hurt you any way he can. He thinks he's some sort of person above the laws others need to follow."

"I got that too. But as of now, he can not only not get into my office, but the clone of the computers, all of them, are now shut off. John, my computer friend, said that Warren even had his computer rigged up so that he could watch people from his home. He had a camera set up on his so he could actually see you guys when you went in and out of the bathroom. Not inside, but it might as well have been for what you could see when the door opened."

"I figured as much. Are you going to fire him? Soon?" He told her that he was, but was waiting to find out who else was in on his little scheme. "Everyone, I would imagine. There are few people on the lines that aren't into him for something. Blackmail, I guess. It's what he had me for. He knows who I am and that I'm running."

"I know some about that as well." Laci nodded and leaned back on the bed. She looked defeated at that moment. "Murph...Phillip said you know her. Can you tell me how?"

"She's run me out of a couple of buildings since I've been here. My aunt won't let me stay with her, even though I set it up for her to be there. She's a stingy bitch too, and I don't know why I ever let her stay with me." Andrew watched her eyes flutter closed as she spoke. "Murph told me once that she could get me in the shelter downtown, but that I'd have to be investigated first. I guess they're really picky about the people they let in."

"They are." Andrew knew that she was falling asleep and he thought it the sexiest thing he'd ever seen. "I'm going to take you home with me. I need to keep you safe."

"All right." Her yawn and smile had him thinking she was only about half listening to him. "It's been so long since I've slept in a bed. Who knew that it could be so relaxing? Oh, and the sex helped too, I suppose. But I'm so tired right now."

He was still smiling twenty minutes later when he called his mom. She said she'd go and look at the address that Kendra had set up for him. He'd realized after Kendra left that he had no idea where his new home was, but he had felt something in his pocket and pulled out a piece of paper with the address on it, then the initial K on at the bottom. His mom laughed before speaking again.

"Are you all right, Andrew? I know that she's still there, at the hospital, but I was wondering if you'd like to bring her over for dinner tonight. I've talked to Misha and Hannah, and they think it might be better if we sort of spaced out our meeting her. We don't want to overwhelm her too much." Andrew laughed and told her that he was pretty sure that just being the two of them was too much for her. "I heard about that dreadful man that hit her. I do hope you break his other jaw. The nerve of some people."

He wanted to point out that she'd been mad at him a little while ago, but decided that he'd be healthy longer if he were to just let it go. His mom was his mom and there wasn't anything he wouldn't do for her. But he was no less afraid of her.

Andrew looked at Laci as she slept and thought of all the times that Warren had more than likely threatened her before this. He was going to make the man pay, that much he knew. When his mom asked him again about dinner, he told her fine but he'd have to ask Laci how she was feeling first.

"She's sleeping right now. And I'm not sure what she has in the way of clothing. The ones she had on when she got here are in a bag for her, but I think they might be ruined. And I didn't see any in her bag that Phillip picked up for her either." His mom asked him if he wanted her to go shopping for her. "I don't think so. I don't know her that well, but I have a feeling that she has tastes in clothing not at all like yours. She's more...I think she's more eclectic. Like she wears what she likes and to hell with convention."

After telling his mom that he'd talk to her when she reported in about his new home, he put his phone away. Andrew was just about to make a couple more calls, one to his attorney and the other to his banker, when Laci woke again.

"I keep dozing off." Andrew told her that was fine. He loved watching her sleep. "Oh sure, that's a lot of fun, watching me snore. Don't you have to go to work or something? I mean, you have to have something better to do than hang out here. Don't you want to go and hang around with Blair? I'm sure he'd just enjoy that to no end."

"No, I don't think either of us would enjoy that. But I don't have a thing to do actually. And my job is sort of in limbo right now. I suppose I could be packing up my apartment, but I have an idea that's been taken care of as well. And before I forget, my mom invited us over to my brother's house. She's living there with them and I told her that I'd speak to you first." Laci told him she didn't know her. "I know. What better time than now to get to? My brothers have been uninvited. She was afraid that they'd overwhelm you."

"Everything about you guys overwhelms me, in case you didn't get that. But I don't understand what this is about." He asked her what she meant. "I mean, you're acting like we're a couple or something. We can't be. I'm not like you."

"I should hope not. I don't think making love would be that much fun if you were." Her face flared up again. "Christ, seeing you all embarrassed makes my dick hard. I would love to make love to you again. Right now."

Had she not looked at his cock, he might have been able to resist her. But her mouth opened just slightly and her body seemed to warm for him. Moving to the bed, he reached for her hand and put it over his cock. As he rocked into her warmth, he told her what he wanted to do to her.

"My cat wants to eat you." Her hand jerked back, but he pulled it back to his cock. "He won't hurt you. He wants to feel you coming down his throat too. His tongue can lap you in ways that I can't, and I think you'll enjoy it."

"I'd rather you did it." He nodded and moaned when she opened the top buttons on her gown and exposed her breasts for him. "I love the way you suck my nipples. The way you nibble on them until I'm so close that I think I could come only from that."

"Show me. Take it completely off and let me see all of you." The sheet was once again on the floor, her gown with it. And when she cupped her breasts in her hands and moaned, Andrew freed his cock and then took off his shirt. His cat, never one to be left out when there was some fun to be had, moved along his skin quickly. Andrew knew that he'd not be able to hold him much longer and pulled his pants off and left them where they lay. "I can't wait, baby. He wants you too."

Andrew pulled Laci to the edge of the bed, her legs dangling off it. When she reached for him, her hands brushing over his aching cock, he kissed her hand and put it beside her on the bed. Andrew kissed her then and let his cat take him.

She didn't run. Nor did she scream like he had expected her to. Andrew knew he was taking the coward's way out of showing her that he was indeed a cat, but he needed her to understand. With his paws on either side of her, his head was level with hers and she only watched him. Andrew dropped to the floor and sat down.

"You're really a cat." He nodded and she giggled. Not the kind of giggle you would expect when something happened that was funny. But more of a nervous kind of I've-gone-over-the-deep-end sort of giggle. "I'm afraid, if you want to know the truth."

He wants you. Her legs closed, and Andrew's cat licked her knees. When she moved, opening her legs to no doubt move away, his cat moved in. Licking her from gate to clit before she could move again, his cat seemed to be pleased with their mate and purred. Her nervousness had the cat in him looking up at him. *Give yourself to him. He wants to drink from you so that he has your scent in his body. And he loves you.*

His cat was gentle with her, bringing her to peak several times before he laid his head on her thigh. She didn't move him off her, nor did she move her leg, but they both seemed to be content with watching each other. And when his cat lifted his head and licked her thigh, she nodded once and he bit her.

Laci watched his cat. She even put her hand in his fur and held him to her. And when he lifted his head, licking the wound closed this time, his cat let him go and Andrew stood over her.

"Take me. Please." He moved between her legs and lifted them up so that her feet were at his shoulders. Sliding into her, feeling her tightness around him, Andrew took her slowly, being as gentle with her as his cat had been. "Please, don't leave me."

"Never." He could see the tears in her eyes, and letting go of her legs so that she could wrap them around his hips, he held her to him, kissing her face, neck, and shoulders while he took her higher and higher. "I love you, Laci. I know that you can't love me yet. But I—"

"It...I think I love you too." Andrew held her to him, taking her harder now, his body needing to claim her again. "You marked me. Bite me again and mark me, Andrew. Please?"

He licked her shoulder to her pulse. He sucked at the heat there, knowing that her blood would be all the riper for her climax, her skin covered in her dew. When she cried out that she was coming, her nails digging into his back, Andrew bit her, feeling his cat helping him. And when he released his own orgasm inside of her, Andrew thought he saw stars and held her closer when he came a second time when she bit into his shoulder.

Holding her now, not having the energy or the willpower to get up, Andrew thought about how his life was going to change. He'd been around his brothers enough to know that this was as enviable as breathing, finding a mate and letting them into your heart. And that was just where Andrew wanted her to be.

CHAPTER 5

The house — was really an understatement to call it something so mundane as a simple house — was beautiful. It hurt her head to think she was going to be staying here with Andrew. Even the furniture — which he claimed he'd had no say in — was just what she would have picked for herself had she the money to do so.

"What do you think?" Laci looked around the huge room they were in...the dining room. Or in this case, what was called a dining room. The room looked nearly as large as some larger restaurants that she'd worked in. "We can change whatever you don't like. I just want to say again that Kendra did this for us, and she won't mind at all."

"The queen." He nodded. Andrew had been telling her about all the people in his life, and her head was beginning to spin with it. "This room is lovely. Just like the rest of the house. You act like you've never seen it before."

"I haven't. I live...lived in an apartment until this morning." Laci nodded. She was homeless up until an hour ago too. "Laci, I know that this is a bit much, but I have to tell you something else. I can read your mind. All of us can.

And I'm not sure, but I think it's a good possibility that you can read ours as well."

She didn't say anything. Not that she didn't believe him...with all the shit going on right now, there was no reason for her not to believe him. But what did you say to a man who professed that he loved you, was a leopard that could read minds, and had told you that you were going to be living in his grand house for the rest of your life?

"The next thing you'll be telling me is that I'm going to live forever." When he didn't laugh or make a comment, Laci turned to him. "I'm not, am I? Going to live forever? And even if I am, could you not tell me right now? I mean, yay, I'm going to live forever, but I don't think I can take too much more change in my life at the moment."

The woman, Emma Rutledge, who had met them at the door, cleared her throat. Laci wasn't sure what she was doing here. She'd told her that she came with the house. Came with the house like she was a stick of furniture that needed to be dusted. Laci had an insane thought as to whether or not she preferred lemony or plain polish when Andrew laughed.

"Miss, there is a gentleman at the door that claims to have a letter for you." Laci backed away from the woman and looked at Andrew. "He said that he's been looking for you for some time. That he has this letter for you and only you."

"I don't want it." Miss Rutledge nodded and started to back out of the room when Laci stopped her. "Did he say who it was from? Or how he found me?"

"No, miss. He only said that he's been looking for you." Miss Rutledge looked at Andrew, then back at her. "He can't come into the house without a proper invite."

"I'll come to see him." Miss Rutledge moved out of the room, and Andrew took her into his arms. He spoke to her in low tones, almost as if he were afraid that she was going to freak out. "He's a vampire. He's fairly old, I think. And pretty powerful. He has no ill will in his heart, only to do what he's been told, and as far as that goes, I can't see what that is beyond the letter. If you don't want to see him, then I can send him on his way."

"Is there anyone that is what they appear to be around here?" Laci knew that she sounded slightly panicky but let him hold her. "I don't know if I even know anyone that's human anymore."

"You know a few that I know of. They smell of you. Not physical contact, but more of a passing one." She looked up at him. "The people you work with, they're all human. Warren is human too. There are a few other shifters at the company, but there are more people like me than you think. After a while, like most shifters, you'll be able to tell the difference. And if you ever want me to change you, then—"

"Not ready for that just yet. But these other people, you can smell them on me." He nodded and backed up a step. "Are you by chance afraid of me?"

"Just a little. You look like you're a little on edge." She told him that she was a lot on edge. "Yeah, I got that too. While you can't kill me, you look like you'd give it your best shot about now."

"I can't take too much more. I feel like that rabbit and the hole he fell into." Andrew said he understood. "No, I don't think you do. I've been leading a normal life up until that fateful day when I only went to the store for some milk. And I've been thinking on that too. I think she had something to do with it. I don't know why but...my aunt must have been pouring it in the sink when I left for work, so I'd have to get it for her. Then all of the sudden, there was a robbery—or what I thought was a robbery—and men were shooting at me and telling me that they've come to get me. Not just a woman, but me by name." Andrew said nothing but she could tell that he was tense. "He called me by my name, not miss or lady, but Laci Wintermute. I thought for sure that my aunt had given it to him, but then he said that they were there to get me and the robbery was going to make for good cover."

"What happened to your aunt? Did they try to get her? Or to hold her hostage so that you'd come to them to get her?" She'd wondered about that as well. How her aunt had been just there, sitting in the aisle waiting for her. The cart she'd been pushing around nowhere in sight. She told Andrew that. "So she was neither shot nor was she hurt. And you brought her with you when you left town."

"She's my aunt." It was lame, even to her ears, why the old biddy was still with her. "I don't know what would have happened to her if I had left her behind."

Nothing, her mind screamed at her. Not a damned thing. Andrew paced the large room but said nothing more. She had her own demons to deal with concerning her aunt, and she wasn't going to talk to him about them right now.

"This vampire. What are we going to do about him?" Andrew looked at her, then at the doorway. "I'm serious, Andrew. I really don't think I can take much more today. Or the rest of the year, as a matter of fact. If he shows his fangs or whatever, I'm going to stake him, then run screaming in the night for any other creature to get me. It'll probably be a giant werewolf, and he'll cut me down before I get ten feet."

"I personal know several. James Luna, for one. But he's a friend of the family. He'd never hurt you. His wife is a lovely woman by the name of Ruby. You'll love her too." He was pacing again and she was sure that he didn't realize what he'd said. There were fucking werewolves too? Laci sat down, then stood up. She was out the door to the main hall before he caught up with her. The man standing at the door smiled at her, without showing any of his teeth.

"What the fuck do you want? And if you so much as mention biting me, I will tear your head off and pee down your neck hole." The man glanced behind her, then at her again. She knew that Andrew was there, but he was staying back. "What's this about a letter you have? Just put it on the floor and kick it this way."

"You're nothing like what I expected. Not timid, nor are you intimidated. Much anyway." She asked him again about the letter. "I'm under orders, you might say. It's to be handed to you. By my own hand."

"Well that's not going to fucking happen, in the event you didn't get that by now. I'm not going anywhere near you without a stake in my hand and a string of garlic. Does that even work?" Both Andrew and the man said no at the same time. "Figures. My life is going to shit every second I'm standing here. Nothing about my life has been right. You should know that I'm on the very edge of getting a gun and blowing every person I see up. Not really, but I'm stressed out. Now tell me or move on, I really could care less at this point."

The man laughed and then bowed. "You are a rare treat in an otherwise sad world. My name is Cyrus. I have no use for a last name, but should you call to my lady Sina or her mate Nildale, I'm sure they can vouch for me. But as I have said, I have this letter for you and you only. It has been...commanded of me that I make sure that you have it."

Before she could ask who they might be, two people were standing in front of her. Laci fell back on her ass and stayed there. If they were going to kill her, then she'd just as soon be close to the floor when she died. Then when another man came in the room, this one dressed in an outfit that made her think of science fiction movies where body armor was made of softer shit, she closed her eyes. When someone touched her shoulder, she sobbed.

"Please don't hurt Andrew. He's a really nice guy. A little on the strange side, but all together nice." She heard someone laugh and opened one eye to look at the woman. "You look like a fashion model. Not that it makes you any less scary, but you're beautiful."

"As are you, Laci Lanning. Come now, get up and let us properly introduce you to ourselves. I'm Sina, second queen. But right now I'm working as queen. My daughter is on an adventure." Laci nodded. "This is my mate, Nildale. He's helping me while she's away. I must say, it's been much harder than I remember it being. And this gentleman here is our son, Nic. He's been working the estate, getting it squared away for Andrew here. But we have come to see you and to clear up any kind of confusion about young Cyrus here."

"If you can clear up even one tenth of the confusion I have, I'll be greatly indebted to you." Nildale moved toward her as he laughed and put out his hand for her. "If you touch me, and I'm not saying you can or not, what happens to me? I mean, I'm new to this whole...I have no idea what you'd call this, but I'm learning shit that is making me a little leery of everyone. But I have a feeling that anything and everything should be questioned. Or just ignored. Which is it?"

"As you should be leery of things. But I only wish to help a lovely young woman from the floor, and to assure you that Cyrus here is truly a friend to us all." Laci eyed his outstretched hand, then him. "You aren't very trusting, are you? I do assure you, I'm not going to harm you in any way that will not benefit you."

She touched her hand to his. By the time what he was saying registered, she felt as if her arm had been set on fire and it was burning down her body. Screaming at the pain of it, she held onto the man that had caused it and screamed again when he was suddenly jerked from her.

~~~

Nic wanted to laugh. It was painful not doing so, but he was barely holding onto his humor. Every time he looked at his father, his back so flat to the floor that he looked as if he might be trying to merge into it, Nic had to work all the harder at not laughing. He was sure it was the cat, his massive jaws around his father's throat, that had him staying as still as he could. Nic tried again to speak around the laughter bubbling up when his sisters came into the room, both Linyah and Kendra. Linyah started laughing almost as soon as she saw him, and it was all it took to bring him over the edge too.

"Would someone like to tell me what in the blazing hells of Madeally is going on?" Kendra looked at him, and he could only point to Laci, then back at his dad and Andrew. "That is not helping. Should I get help?"

"No. No, I don't think Andrew needs any help." Nic laughed harder when he saw his dad's face. "I'm pretty sure that he has it under control."

"Nic. Behave." He tried to for his mom, but he was going to hurt himself. With a final look from his mom that said he'd pay, she continued. "Your father thought he'd be clever and give young Laci here a bit of his magic. He actually told her that he'd not hurt her. Well, as you can see, he did, and Andrew took exception to that. Poor dear. I bet she never lets any of us hug her again. And I've so come to enjoy it when one of you would just wrap me up in their arms."

Laci struggled to stand, and Nic moved to help her. "Don't touch me. I think I could go for the rest of my life without any of you touching me again. Christ, what the fuck was that?"

"Magic." Laci glared at him as she made her way to Andrew. When she wrapped her arms around his waist, Nildale whimpered. Nic walked to the couple and his dad again. "He's hurting him. While he cannot kill him, he can still cause him a great deal of pain."

"Yeah, well, he can suffer a bit longer." Nic said nothing, but he knew that the couple were talking. And when Andrew let his dad go, Nic helped his dad to stand up. Laci looked at his dad. "You should be beaten. All of you. You lied to me. And hurt me. Why? What did I ever do to you? Nothing. That's what. I did nothing to you."

"I am profoundly sorry, my child. If I had thought this through, I would have known that as a newly mated couple he would have been on the defense." Nic watched his dad put out his hand. "Will you forgive an old man who only thought to help you out?"

"Not yet. And if you think I will ever let you touch me again, you're nuttier than my aunt." He looked pained, but his dad nodded and stepped back from Laci. Nic wanted to tell her that he'd never hurt her again, but his mom spoke through their link.

Don't. This is between them, and your father should have known better than to do such a stupid thing. Nic agreed with his mom but told her that dad was hurt. *And you don't think that she is? She trusted him and he hurt her. Laci will forgive him, but she needs this as much as he does. Andrew will feel badly for this as well. He hurt a friend of his.*

Nic knew that his mom was right, but he didn't have to like it. He turned to the front door when someone cleared their throat. Christ, he'd forgotten about Cyrus. The big vampire was smiling when Nic walked to him.

"You have quite a family here, Nic. Why have I not noticed that before?" Nic told him he wasn't around enough. "True. But my kind causes more grief than it does happiness. People are simply too afraid of me. Then there is my master. He is not a man that should be trusted even with his own mother, I think."

"You're harmless for the most part." Cyrus said nothing. "Andrew lives here. He's gone to get dressed with his mate. I'm sorry, but I can't invite you in."

"No harm. I was entertained. The young human…your father did right by what he did for her. In the coming weeks, days I would think, things are going to come to a head for her, and she will need the boost he has given her." Nic asked him what he meant. "I cannot tell you, my friend. You know that as well as I. My soul is no longer mine, and I must do the bidding of one that holds me."

"I can still talk to my family for you. You know that they'd do anything for you." Cyrus shook his head, and Nic felt his pain. "You're here for him then? He has a letter for Laci."

"I do and he does. I am sorry about this. I have no say over what he commands me to do." Nic nodded and turned when Andrew came into the hall with Laci. "When I have gone, will you please explain to them? I should like to, someday if it is possible, come back to talk to them. When there are no ill feelings between us."

"I will."

Cyrus nodded and smiled at Laci. Nic looked at her too and wondered if she had any idea what or even how much magic his dad had given her. He was sure that Cyrus did as well as the rest of them, but Laci was going to have to learn.

Then Nic had a thought. Did his dad know what was coming?

"My lady." Cyrus bowed before Laci, and she took a step back from the door. The vampire nodded as if he understood and had expected the shun, but only smiled at her. "I have a letter for you. It is from my sire."

"Your father? I don't know who that is. Why would he — ?" Andrew must have told her because she became embarrassed and told Cyrus she was sorry. "I'm new to this whole magic stuff. And shifters and things like that in general. Please forgive me. But I still have no idea who your maker is. Nor why he would be writing to me."

"I am but the messenger my lady, please remember that when you read this." Cyrus looked at Andrew as he continued. "Might I suggest that you do not invite me in? I should like to be within the warmth of your family if only for a moment, but I think it best that you do not. My intentions are not worthy today. I have been set on a task that is not of my making, and I don't know what will happen once she has touched this letter. The magic on it is connected to me somehow, I think."

"He wants you to hurt her. Or something else." Cyrus held out the envelope and said nothing. Andrew nodded and spoke again. "I will kill you if this causes any harm to her. I'm a mite on edge today, what with all that has been going on lately. So as you said, you aren't worthy today and you try anything, I will kill you."

"And I would not fight you. Life since I have been awakened has not been what I had expected. My past is...gone for me." Nic watched the two men, and when Laci took the envelope, he was almost afraid for her. Cyrus spoke again, quietly this time. "Careful, my lady. Once opened it cannot be closed again."

"I'm not going to open it at all. You delivered it under duress, right?" Cyrus nodded. "Well, you did your part. Now I'm going to do mine."

When she asked for a lighter, his dad came forward and put out his hand. There was a flame in his palm and Laci only stared at it for several seconds before she started to put the letter in it. But she looked at Cyrus again.

"You should go now. I don't want him to ask you if I read it or something and you have to lie." Cyrus told her that he couldn't lie to his master. "Oh. Well, you should go anyway. What you don't see for sure, you won't have to tell him, correct?"

Cyrus smiled. "You are much more brilliant than he believes you to be. Nay, I cannot tell him what I do not know." He bowed before her again. "I am in your debt, my lady. So long as I live."

"And I yours." He started to fade out, but she called him back. "Cyrus, if you need me or anyone in this family for any reason, call to us. We will help you as you have me today. Because even though I only just met you, I don't think you're as bad as the man that holds you right now."

After he was gone, Nic looked at Laci with new eyes. He was sure that she had no idea what she'd just done. Or what gift had been given to her from Cyrus. The trust of a vampire and a promise. She too had given Cyrus more in these last few minutes than he'd had in all of his dark existence.

"This envelope? What kind of shit might be in it?" Nic told Laci that he had no idea. "But you're sure, like I am, that whatever is in it, it's going to be bad. And that, like he said, if I open it, it's a done deal?"

"Yes." She looked at the envelope and Nic spoke softly to her. "Cyrus works for and is commanded by a powerful and old vampire. He is...let's just say that he is on the verge of his peers doing something about him. His name is Martin, and he is known for his cruelty as well as his sadistic ways. When Cyrus returns to him, and he has no choice in the matter, he will pay for not coming into the house and doing to you whatever he was told. At great risk to himself, he has saved you."

"I'm going to help him. I don't know how, but I'm going to. He didn't just save me, but he also saved this family if I'm not mistaken. Being invited into this home would have given him access to them all, wouldn't it?" Nic nodded, impressed more so by her thinking. Laci looked at his dad again. "I'm still not very happy with you, but if I burn this in your hand, will you be hurt? I don't want anyone to be injured because of this."

"Nay, I will not be harmed. His magic, whatever it might be, cannot do anything to me." Laci asked his dad if she would be hurt. "I will not allow that either. My flame, and the magic with it, is stronger than anything he could make. Even should it be something from Sonya, it will have no effect on anyone here."

The envelope touched the flame and it burned red. The magic in it, unstable because it had not been used properly, burned hotly then was gone. The ash, red like blood, lay on his dad's palm for several seconds before it too disappeared as the envelope had.

"Dad?" Kendra looked at him when his dad was so still. "Dad, what is it? What did it say?"

It wasn't until his mom walked over and touched his arm that his dad came out of the trance-like state he'd been in. His face was unreadable, but his stiff body wasn't. Whatever had been in the envelope had not been anything good. And when he took Mom into his arms and held her tightly, Nic found himself stiffen, readying for whatever happened next.

"You were right not to read it." Laci nodded while his dad explained. "Had you done so, even with the bit of magic that I gave you, you would have suffered horribly. And one who touched you to render aid would have suffered as well. Sonya has hired Martin to keep you from breeding...having a child. She thought that a union between you and Andrew would be stronger than anything we have seen so far, and that a child between the two of you would be stronger still."

"She wanted me dead so I'd not have a baby? How fucking sick is this bitch? And where is she?" His dad explained that she was dead. "And yet she still pisses me off. What kind of things did that man have to do to me? He said that the magic was attached to him. What would me reading this or even opening the envelope have done to him?"

His dad looked around. Nic thought perhaps he wasn't going to answer her. Or maybe he didn't want to. But when he held Mom in his arms again, Nic wasn't even sure he wanted to know. And he'd been around a very long time and had seen things that would have killed a lesser man.

"Cyrus was to rape you, here in this house while Andrew watched. Not only unable to come to your aid, but none of us could have. Then when he was finished, he was to dismember you, in small enough pieces, mind you, that he could then feed you to your mate and there would have been nothing he could have done about it." Laci leaned into Andrew as his dad continued. "The magic that was there would have allowed the vampire to not only do as he was told, but it would have commanded him to do these things to you without his consent. When he returns to his master, he will be most displeased with him."

"Can I save him?" Nic started to tell her that was a bad idea when Dad said that she could. "How? How can I save this man from the monster that created him?"

"Martin did not create young Cyrus. That is important for you to know. But as for Martin, you must kill him." Laci stared at him, waiting like the rest of them for Dad to tell her how to do that. "The magic that you have now, it's very powerful. Much stronger than the monster that owns Cyrus. Call to him. Once he is here, kill him."

Before Nic could tell her again what a bad idea this was, Misha appeared in the room. The man looked frantic, his dress sloppy. Nic drew his swords, as did his father and mother.

"It's time. The baby. It's coming. Hurry." He stood there for several seconds and looked ready to fall apart when Misha spoke again. "Christ. I'm going to be a dad soon."

CHAPTER 6

Andrew paced. And when he sat down, one of his brothers began the short trip up and down the small room. It felt as if they'd been here for hours, but he knew, after consulting his watch for the tenth time in as many minutes, it had only been less than one. But that made it no less scary for the time.

"She's going to be just fine." He nodded at his mom. "Do sit down, Andrew. You're wearing a hole in the floor. And please tell your brothers to do the same."

Max was the only one that was sitting quietly. The women, including Laci, had gone down to the cafeteria, as well as a quick stop at the gift shop. Thomas was looking like a man who was going to a firing squad. Rider had long since left them to pace the hallway and to bother the nurses at the desk every two minutes. Carter was sitting on the edge of his seat like at any moment he was going to get up and resume the path he'd been taking. And Phillip was turning the pages of a magazine. He knew that he hadn't seen a single thing in the stupid book because he'd been dividing his glaring between the clock and the door. Andrew went to sit with Max.

"You nervous?" He said that he was not. "You know something that we should know? I mean, like the baby is going to be born soon?"

"He'll be here soon. I don't think there is very much choice in the matter, do you?" Andrew laughed when he did. "The baby and mother are fine. Hannah is moving along nicely and the little boy will be born when he comes into the world. I can't tell the time because I've had little contact with him."

"You can talk to the babies?" Max told him that they all could if they listened. "I'm not sure what I'd even say to a baby. Can they even understand us?"

"They understand love, hate. Even when they are not wanted. The little boy, he knows that he's going to be loved and taken care of. And he's just as nervous as the rest of you about coming into the world." Andrew wasn't sure about that. He wasn't so much nervous as he was terrified as to what the baby would be like.

Instead of getting up to pace again, he leaned back on the seat and tried to get his mind to relax. He thought of the store that his brother Carter and he were going to open in a few weeks. Bits and Pieces was set to open on the first of April. Yes, he'd not been thrilled about the date and what it implied, but Carter thought that with it being the first, they'd get more people coming in that were curious than anyone who wanted to make fun of them. Sounded like a plan.

Inventory had started coming in yesterday. Boxes and boxes of leather straps, buttons as well as hinges and pieces of glass for glass work. Then there had been the scavenger's hunts that the two of them had been on. He thought perhaps that had been the most fun.

Going to garage sales, auctions, and even tag sales, they'd picked up broken furniture, parts to things they had no idea what it had been used for. Chandeliers and stained glass items. All for the parts, even some boxes and crates of odds and ends that had specialty pieces in them, like keys and drawer pulls. They'd even begun to collect doors with handles on them that were nearly as beautiful as the wood they were in.

Just an hour ago he'd been notified that someone had a house full of furniture that they wanted to sell. Most of it, he'd been told, was out of shape. Some of it only had the legs to a sofa or the drawers all gone from a cabinet. They would take Max with them when they went to see if there were things he could sell in his own antique shop.

"Mom is going to talk to Laci today about working for me." Andrew said he'd mentioned it a couple of times too. "She will be great. Aunt Laci can sell anything, I think. I've heard about her sales commissions."

"I'm getting it all returned to her. I can't take it from those that benefited from it, but I'm getting all of hers returned to her. It amounted to several thousand dollars." Max nodded. "Why Laci, Max? Why do you want her to come and work for you? Murph said you had it in your head she was going to even before she became a part of our family."

"I don't know." Andrew said he didn't believe that. "There are things that I can see that are as clear as day. Not a lot of things, but things that are coming or going to happen to someone. But then there are things that I can only see parts of. Segments of something coming, but not necessarily who or what. And when it's about me or my mom, it's murky and unclear. Frustrating actually. Grandma thinks it's because I can change it if I need to. But I'm not sure how that would work either."

"This thing with the vampire, do you know how it ends?" Max said that he didn't, but he knew that Cyrus wasn't going to hurt anyone. "But this other guy, Martin, his master, he will?"

"I believe that he will try. Other than that, I'm not really sure. I do know that he and Aunt Laci have a sort of showdown. But the outcome? I don't know. And as Grandpa Nildale said, he is not his maker. I don't know why yet, but that is important. Grandma told me that since you've bonded with Aunt Laci that she can't be killed like other humans would be, which will be good." Max sat there for several seconds. "Do you think she can summon him here? Aunt Laci. I mean, to where she is? I think I'd like to see that. Maybe when she does it she can make sure that I'm not in bed."

Andrew started to tell him that he'd wake him for that, but he saw Misha coming down the hall. He wasn't so much walking as he was sort of dancing. Andrew smiled. Misha's son was here. And when they all stood up, he picked up their mom and swung her around the room, laughing. Sitting her down, he held her close to him and looked at them.

"It's a boy and he's perfect." He handed him his cell phone, and Andrew saw the little face before the others started crowding around him. "Nine pounds four ounces and nineteen inches long. All his fingers and toes too." He kissed Mom again. "Hannah is doing great. The doctor told us he'd never had such a wonderful delivery and said he'd bring all our children into the world."

He looked pretty good. Even the shots of Hannah holding her son were good, if not a little blurry. Andrew supposed that he'd not be any better. It was a very emotional time for all of them. The phone was passed along to the others, and he hugged Misha when his turn came and felt the love of family stronger in that moment than he had his whole life. Then the others showed up, and it was a Lanning free for all.

Laci stayed back at first. When the hugs started to include wives of his brothers, she even tried to hide behind him. But Misha wasn't having it. They were family, he told her, and she was now a part of it. Andrew's cat didn't even get pissy when Misha kissed her on the cheek. Andrew was glad that they were all there for this, and was thankful that everything had turned out well for his brother and sister-in-law.

Crowding into the room later, when Hannah had been put in her own room, they all hugged her as well. Andrew noticed that his mom kept touching the new baby but not picking him up. He went to stand by her when she put her hands behind her back.

"Just pick him up." She shook her head. "Well if you don't, I'm going to. I want to feel him in my arms, and I know that you do."

"I do but...well, it's been a really long time, Andrew. I'm not sure of all the rules just yet." He asked her what rules. "Oh my goodness, there are so many now days. Did you know that they don't use powder on babies anymore? Not even when you take them out of the bath. And soap? There are special soaps that you use on babies now that I've never heard of. What if they have a special way of holding them now? What if I mess up?"

Misha stepped to the little cradle and picked up the baby before he could tell his mom what a crock of shit that was. He wasn't sure, but thought that Mom had used powder on them as well as any soap that had been on the market. None of them had any kind of reaction that he knew of.

Misha held out his son to Mom. "Mom, I'd like for you to meet your second of many grandchildren. His name is Kelly James Lanning, my son." When she seemed hesitant about taking him, Andrew gave her a little push. "You don't want to hold him?"

"I do. I really do." When she took him in her arms, Kelly opened his eyes and looked right at her. Andrew noticed that he had the most startling blue eyes that he'd ever seen. Even more brilliant than Misha's. "Oh Misha, he looks so much like you did. Maybe even prettier."

"He's handsome, not pretty, Mom. Boys are handsome." Mom nodded at Misha as she pulled the blue bonnet off Kelly's head. "Hannah was surprised by how much hair he has. And Daniel too. He said that he'd never seen a newborn that might need a haircut in a couple of days."

It was long and thick. Andrew touched his own fingers to the top of his little head and thought it was at least three to four inches long, and as curly as he'd seen Hannah's be when she let it down. The little guy was going to be a big hit with the women when he got older, Andrew was almost afraid to see him grow up.

"I'm so glad you named him for his grandmother. The poor dear missed so much. I'll have to do double duty now, I suppose." Misha laughed when Andrew did at his mom's proclamation. "When is Carole going to get here, do you know?"

"She's on her way now. I guess there were a couple of things she wanted to finish up before coming back. The house is sold now, and she's got the business running the way she wants again as well." Andrew asked if she was going to stay here on a permanent basis. "Yes. Other than traveling back and forth to her company, I think she's done with the other stuff. Not having Howard keeping her locked away, Carole has been blooming I guess. Her husband should have died a long time ago."

Andrew couldn't have agreed more. Kelly Little, Hannah's mom, had been killed when Hannah had been born. Then Hannah had been kidnapped by the murderer and had spent her life being abused. After it was discovered who her grandparents were, arrangements were made for them to meet, but her grandfather, Howard, had other plans in mind when he came to see his only granddaughter. Andrew was glad that things had worked out.

He found Laci sitting with Max and Murph and wondered what sort of trouble they were up to now. When Laci looked up at him, Andrew thought that he could gladly leave all of this, find a nice dark room, and make her scream out his name over and over. He was just going to suggest that when she stood up and moved toward him. Andrew followed her when she took his hand and led him out of the room.

~~~

Martin was pissed. But he thought, for now anyway, that he was holding onto his rage pretty well. The worthless piece of shit in front of him hadn't given him what he wanted. And Martin thought by now, everyone would know that he always got what he wanted.

"You gave it to her, the envelope that I gave you, you handed it to Laci?" He said that he had. Several times now, but he wasn't getting the answers that he wanted and he was pretty sure that Cyrus knew it. "Then why am I not happy with the results? She was to die. By your hand. The spell in that envelope was there so that you'd be responsible for her murder and no one would connect it to me. Tell me what you did. What happened?"

"I do not know, my lord. I handed it to her as you said for me to, then I left." Martin lashed out at Cyrus and was pissed when he didn't whimper or cry out when his magic tore into his flesh. "My lord, you are aware, are you not, that Lady Sonya is dead?"

Martin knew that. It had been all over the magical world that the great and powerful Sonya had been murdered for no reason. Well, Martin thought there might have been one or two reasons that the queen had killed her, but he didn't think she should have died like she had. To have been burned to death by her own magic.... Well, Martin was going to have a care from now on who he pushed his magic at. There was no point in getting himself hurt. And now with Sonya out of the way, he could move into her territory and take over where she had failed and make it his own.

"Sonya was a great lost to us all." He looked around the room at his servants, daring any of them to gainsay him. "She was a great lost to us all, was she not?"

Every one of them nodded, like puppets with strings. Martin looked at the bleeding body before him and was disgusted. No one was going to think they were more magical than him, and no one more powerful when it came to ruling his people. Martin ruled not with an iron fist but one made of diamonds and stone. He knew those things were much stronger than a simple metal, like iron.

Now what to do about Cyrus. He couldn't kill him. He wanted to, almost on a daily basis, but it wasn't within his power. Cyrus didn't belong to him. He worked for him, even did his bidding, but Martin hadn't made him. Cyrus only thought he had. And Martin was never going to tell him. If he killed the man before him, then his own master, more powerful and greater than anyone Martin had ever met, would come to him. He'd know where he was and kill him without Martin ever being able to explain himself.

"You're to go to your room and you are not to feed for a week." Cyrus said nothing. Not that he was allowed, but Martin wanted to hear him beg. Or at the very least look up at him with that questioning look he had. "And then, maybe then, I will allow you to come and work for me again. Be gone."

When he simply disappeared, Martin started to stand and see what had happened. There was no way that he'd developed that power. Martin couldn't even do that as yet, and he'd been around for centuries. The art of transportation was something that he'd never been able to conquer. But he would. Martin looked at his harem and decided that he'd treat himself for not murdering Cyrus.

"Come here." Two of the women that he'd changed recently started to back away from him. "I said to come here."

They knew better than to disobey him a second time. Martin didn't like being denied and when he was, he let everyone, even the household, know it. But when they came to him on their knees, Martin was both disappointed and excited to see them with his marks on their backs, blood seeping from the rags that they had been given by him.

After telling them to strip, he watched as they took off the bits of clothing that hid little. Christ, they had wonderful bodies, and he reached down and stroked his cock while he watched. As soon as they were both naked, he ordered them to kiss and fondle each other. He wasn't pleased with them when they shied away from it.

"I said to fuck each other. Now. Suck each other off and then when you come, both of you, I want you to come here to me." The blonde cupped the redhead's tit and he felt his cock stretch. Pulling himself free of his pants, he waited for them to get moving. As soon as Blonde dropped to her knees in front the redhead, he felt his balls tighten up. "That's it. Eat her pussy and fuck her with your fingers."

They were both moaning now. Redhead was cupping her tits and pinching her nipples. Her hips were rocking hard into Blonde's mouth, and he wanted to feel her mouth on his cock. Watch her suck him off while Redhead let him feed from her tits. Martin stroked harder, faster, wanting to have them come once before he had them service him. Not for their pleasure — he could care less if they enjoyed themselves — but he wanted them to think he wasn't going to hurt them again.

When Redhead came, screaming out her release, Martin got up and stood behind her. Taking her tit into his hand, he squeezed it hard enough to have her screaming again, this time in pain. And when he ordered Blonde to get her mouth on his cock, he stood there so that she could while he abused Redhead.

He fucked her mouth hard, not caring at all when she cried out. When she tried to pull away, he grabbed her head with his free hand and jerked her back, shoving his cock hard down her throat. He wasn't large, but he could do a great many things with his cock. Bringing Redhead to his body, he bent her back until he could reach her tit and bit savagely into her, tearing at her tender flesh as he drank greedily. When he felt himself ready to come, his cock buried deep in the hole where it was, he pulled Redhead's throat to his mouth and tore into her vein, blood spilling all over him as he let it wash over him.

When she was near death he let her fall to the floor. Wrapping his hands around Blonde's head, he fucked her like he would a pussy, hard pounding strokes until he emptied himself twice down her gullet. When he was finished, his cock still semi-hard, he turned to the row of men and women that he'd made and ordered one of them to come to him.

A man and a woman came when he ordered it a second time. He was going to have to do something about this. They were not doing as he'd commanded the first time, but for now, he needed relief and knew they were going to die giving it to him. The male held the woman when he told him to and Martin fucked her, the blood from the blonde making the slide easier for him as the woman wasn't enjoying herself enough to give him any kind of slide. The male watched his cock sliding in and out of the woman, and he told him to fuck her too. The two of them were in and out of the woman so fast that Martin could feel his cock brush against the other man's every time he pulled back.

Martin came twice more, his body nearly weak with his releases. But when the man came as well, bringing the woman with him, Martin reached over and snapped his neck, then that of the woman. He'd not given either of them permission to release, so they had to pay the consequences. He staggered back from their bodies and stood there.

He was bathed in blood and his cock was, for now, sated. Martin looked around the room and was disgusted by what he saw. Children, even though they were all adults in age, were children compared to the power he held. No matter how many he changed, no one even came close to giving him what he wanted. Changing people to vampire, he knew, should have given him more. All it did was piss him off.

He called for his servant and when Butler — whatever his name had been…Martin had long since forgotten it — when he came into the room, Martin ordered him to clean up. The rest of his children departed when he waved them away. It was getting late in the morning anyway.

"My lord, Cyrus is missing." He told him he'd sent him to his room. "Nay, my lord, he is no longer on the estate. I went there earlier to see if he could repair one of the lawn mowers for me and he was gone. Even his things are missing."

"Did you check the garage too?" Butler said that he'd checked everywhere that he could think of, but there wasn't any sign of him. "He had better not have. I own him."

Butler said nothing but continued to order the slaves he had to clean up the mess. Blood was staining the carpet, but Martin knew that when he returned there wouldn't be anything to show that he'd had his fun. Getting up from his chair, he manufactured himself clothing as he made his way to Cyrus's room. The fucker had better be where he told him to be.

Not only was the room empty of Cyrus and his clothing as Butler had said, but his scent was gone too. Martin had discovered quite by accident that Cyrus didn't have a scent anywhere but in his rooms. He'd never figured out how that was happening, and he'd never asked Cyrus either. The fact that Martin knew less than them wasn't going to be something that he'd let anyone know about. Martin turned to Butler, who had come with him, when he saw the small envelope on the stand. He picked it up and tore it open before he thought that he shouldn't. The magic hit him right in the face and he fell back to the floor.

When he woke it was light enough in his room that he knew he was in his room, but had no memory of how he'd gotten there. Butler, he thought, or one of the dozens of others that he owned. Rolling to his back, he looked up at the ceiling and tried to retrace his steps. The envelope and thinking about what might have been inside of it had him sitting up on his bed.

"Hello, Martin." The voice was dark, as dark as the room was now. The light that always burned when he slept was out. Not even a little light shone under the door any longer. "You have something that belongs to me. Or you did."

"Who is that? What are you doing in my lair?" Martin heard the chair shift under the person's weight. And even in the darkness he could see movement, feel the darkness take shape and size. When the person was there, within touching distance, Martin leaned back from him. He could also feel the anger and magic from the person. Then the flare of light nearly blinded him.

"No," was all he could manage when he saw who stood before him. "You can't be here. I have magic."

The man laughed, threw back his head, and roared with it. Martin felt his skin crawl, his balls slide up into his body, and his cock shrivel. Christ, he was going to die. And it wouldn't be as quick or as nice as any of Martin's more torturous play times.

CHAPTER 7

Laci wasn't sure what she was doing here, but Max had told her that her aunt had called and demanded that she come to see her. Murph had dropped her off about twenty minutes ago and now she was sitting here in the lobby waiting for her to come and get her.

After giving everything that had happened to her over the last few months a great deal of thought, she knew that somehow her aunt had been playing her. Laci wasn't sure how she might have been involved or even if she was in the robbery in the first place, but she had a feeling she had been. There was a lot of things that had come to light now that she wasn't working herself to death all the time and she was feeling better. And loved.

Looking around the room she was in, Laci wondered what the holdup was. It wasn't as if she had a lot to do today, but she certainly didn't want to have to be sitting here, waiting on her aunt to get her ass in gear. Carter did have good security in place, but she'd been summoned. Why wasn't her aunt letting her go up to see her?

"She's playing this power thing with you." Laci looked at the woman sitting across from her. "None of us care all that much for her, I'm sorry to tell you. Bitchiest woman I done ever did see. Ordering us others around like she's the queen of it all."

"I'm sure she doesn't mean that. She's just used to getting things the way she likes them." The woman snorted at her. "She's had a hard life."

"I'd been living in my car for four years before coming here. Eating from the dumpsters when I could get it, and even stealing when I couldn't get even that. I can tell you about hard life, and that woman don't have nearly what any person would consider hard." Laci knew that too. Her aunt seemed to always have the best of everything. "You keep doing what she tells you and she's gonna suck you dry, see if she don't."

"I promised my father that I'd look after her when he wasn't able to anymore." The woman asked where he was. "He and my mom were killed in a car crash a few years ago. She'd been living with my parents when it happened."

"I'm betting she ain't let up one bit since you been doing it either. Not one time said thank you." Laci said nothing. If anything her aunt was more demanding than before. "You should just go on home and be with that man of yours. He's gonna treat you better on his worst day than she will the rest of her miserable life."

Laci said nothing. She would have rather been with Andrew, but Aunt Jeanie had said it was important. Besides, Andrew and his brothers were unloading boxes at the warehouse he and Carter were using. And when this was done, she had to meet Murph and Max at the shop that they had. The place she might start working at.

When the lady at the front desk told her that her aunt was ready for her, she stood to go up. The woman grabbed her arm and told her to run. It was the strangest thing in the world for someone to say to her, and Laci had the most incredible urge to do just that. Run from here and never to return. But duty called. And even though her aunt was her only living relative, she was duty now.

The elevator up was nice. There were pictures on the walls of it, some of them residents of the building she'd bet, and others of the park outside of it. Flowers and trees were the main subject of the photographer, but there were animals as well. One of them was a great leopard, and Laci knew that it was one of the Lanning men. When the doors yawned open, she hesitated before moving into the hall. She didn't want to be there.

Then you shouldn't be. Andrew. He'd shown her last night how she could speak to him. Well, really he'd shown her what he'd wanted to do to her and with her when they got home. The man did have the best ideas when it came to sex and her. *If you come here now, I'll show you some more things I've been thinking about doing with you.*

I can't. I can't just leave her here. I mean, I should, she's a mean old biddy and I think she's going to try and hit me up for money. I've already decided to tell her that she's on her own. Andrew told her he was proud of her. *Yeah, well, don't congratulate me just yet. She has a tendency to run right over me when she thinks her way is better.*

You'll be just fine. And when you're done telling her off, come here and I'll make sure you know just how proud I am of you. Her body warmed up and she made herself step out of the elevator when the doors started to close. *Good girl. Now go and tell her you're finished with her.*

As she made her way down the long hall, she thought of the money that she had in her new account. Seven grand. All of it hers. And as soon as Blair got back to work, it was going to be his last day. Laci was going to go with Andrew to tell

Blair that he was going to pay it all back to her. She was both afraid and excited at the same time.

Before she could knock on the door it was opened. Not gently either. Her aunt was standing there, her cane in one hand and her other hand hanging onto the door. Laci wanted to turn and leave, but she lifted her chin and stared at her.

"You think this is funny?" Laci asked her what she was talking about. "Making me wait when I know you left that lobby over five minutes ago. And don't be blaming it on the elevator either. I know them things are fast. You should have been here three minutes ago."

Laci wondered how one would time the speed of an elevator, but decided it wasn't worth the effort to know. As far as she was concerned, this was going to be her last time here anyway.

"Well, I'm here now. What is it you want?" Her aunt just glared and moved back to her chair. Laci had often wondered why her aunt had needed such a prop; like a lot of things in her aunt's life, this was for show. Whether for power or just someone to feel sorry for her, the chair, like the cane, wasn't necessary for her aunt to get around. "I have another appointment, so if you can tell me what you wanted, I'll be on my way."

"You'll get your butt in here. And I'll tell you when you can go. There ain't no appointment either. You just ain't that important. You'll tell me what I'm supposed to be doing without any funds to tide me over. My meds are not coming to me like they should be, and I can't get these fools here to go to the store for me either. I'm stuck here." It was on the tip of her tongue to tell Aunt Jeanie to get her own things, but she moved inside the apartment and closed the door behind her. Standing in the little hall, she took a deep breath and let it go with a count of ten. "Get in here, Laci. I swear to you if your father were alive, he'd be very upset with how you're treating me."

"But he's not, and I think I've done well by you. You're the one living in a nice apartment when I was living in an abandoned building. You didn't even want me to come here and take a shower." She sat down on the couch and realized that it was not the one that had been here when she'd brought her aunt to live here. "When did you get this?"

There were other things too. A lamp that hadn't been there before. A desk with a nice laptop on it. Laci got up and moved around the room looking at all the new upgrades that hadn't been a part of the place when she'd first brought her here.

"You leave my things alone. And how I spend my money is my business. Had you not made me leave my other things behind, I'd not have had to buy more. You owe me for that too." Laci turned and looked at her. "I've been keeping track of what I've spent, and you can get it in cash for me. I don't want no check from you that'll probably be no good. Then there are my meds. I can't go and get them, and nobody will deliver them without paying for them up front. Go down there and get them and set up some sort of account with them so I can just have them bill you for when I need them. There are more things too. I need an account set up by you that will get me those things as well. You'll have to just miss work to get all this done for me, because I want it done today."

"No. I'm not going to pay you...how the hell did you afford this anyway? You only have your social security check. Even if you were to have been saving it all, you'd not have the money for this many new things." Aunt Jeanie told her it was none of her business. "Whatever then. And I'm not going to set anything up to pay for them either. If you can have this sort of new things, then you can certainly afford your own meds."

The cane hit the floor hard and Laci decided that she wasn't going to be afraid of her or the threat of the cane any more. As she moved around the room, looking at the new things her aunt had, all she could think about was how she'd had to work several jobs to make it so her aunt could have a home. And come to find out, she not only had a nice home but new furniture as well.

"Laci, I'm not going to stand for this treatment of me. You made a promise to your father that you'd care for me when he passed." Laci said nothing but picked up a framed picture and stared at the man and woman there. How had she not noticed how sad they were before this? "Put that down. That is no concern of yours. Put it back, I said."

Putting it back on the shelf, but not the one it had been on, she stood there thinking. There was so much she wanted to say to her aunt and none of it was going to be nice. But instead of telling her to fuck off—what she wanted to do more than anything—she only nodded and started for the door. Pausing before opening it, she turned back to her aunt.

"I want to tell you something about me. I'm married now. My name is Laci Lanning, if you care. Andrew and I are...well, we're happy. He has this great house that has servants and a cook, and I find that I love the wealthy life." Aunt Jeanie told her that she lied. "No. I'm not lying. We live in this beautiful mansion that has ten bedrooms and more land than I've ever been on before. A pool...well, all kinds of things that I love. Not as much as I do Andrew, but I do like having nice things."

"He's not going to keep you around. Just look at you. You don't even know how to dress nicely. Not that I believe you, but you're nothing but trash and you always will be."

Laci said nothing, but smiled. "I want you to take care of my needs if you're so rich now, Laci. I'm not going to be calling you to get yourself here whenever I have something for you to do. The account at the pharmacy and the grocery, as well as someone to come and clean up my place. And you might as well have someone to cook for me too. You get that taken care of today and then come back here and give me the money I had to spend on this hole you dumped me in."

Laci moved back in the room and skirted around her aunt. She was sure that she thought she'd won, and when she smiled at Laci, she felt like a mouse with her the cat. Then she thought of Andrew and the rest of the Lanning family. Picking up the picture in the frame, she put it close to her heart.

"I never got to keep anything of my parents when they died. You told me that there were no pictures of him or Mom left after the sale of their things. You said that the lawyers had taken it all. Why would you lie to me about that?" Aunt Jeanie just glared instead of answering her. "I guess you have your own secrets. But I want you to know that as of right this minute, I'm finished with you. You live here, do whatever it takes for you to get by. But as of now, we're done."

"You'll be done with me when I say you're done. I rule you, not the other way around." Laci laughed as she made her way back to the door. "You will pay for this Laci, see if you don't. And when those men come looking for you again, I'm going to be as rich as you claim you are now."

Laci opened the door when what she'd said occurred to her. Laci turned to look at her aunt and saw the look of triumph on her face. She thought she'd won. Whatever was going on, her aunt had arranged it all.

"What men? You said when those men come looking for me again. You mean the ones from the store? You know them?" Her aunt closed her lips so tightly that Laci knew she was trying hard not answer her. "Max said that I can make it so you can't lie to me. I want you to tell me the truth. Did you know those men who were at the store?"

"Of course I did. They were gonna take you then and I'd be paid. It was supposed to be sooner, right after your parents died. But they kept not coming when they said. I had to keep going there and going there until that day. And you had to screw that up too, didn't you?" Her lips closed again and Aunt Jeanine was fighting hard, but Laci won. "Twice more you had to get in their way on the way here, and twice I had to forfeit a bit of my cash. See if you don't pay me back for that too. But this time they'll get you. I'll make sure of it. I'm sick to death of you anyway."

"Where? Where are they going to try and get me?" Her aunt put her hand over her mouth. Blood seeped between her fingers, and Laci knew that she was biting her lips so she'd not answer her. "Tell me where?"

A power rolled over her. Not like when that man had touched her but gently, like she was being bathed in sunshine and warmth. When Aunt Jeanie took her hand off her mouth, Laci could see that not only had she bitten her lips, but it looked like she'd bitten through them as well.

"The pharmacy. You're to die at the pharmacy." Aunt Jeanie leaned back in her chair as she continued. "Go there, Laci. Go there and let them kill you so I can collect. I want my money."

Laci felt her skin chill and her blood cool in her veins. Her aunt had sold her out. Not once, but several times. She was almost afraid, sickened really, to think that her aunt might have had something done to her parents. Telling her to go to sleep and not to wake until someone knocked on her door and said her name, Laci left the apartment and made her way to the elevator as she reached for Andrew.

~~~

Murph kept a close eye on Laci as they stood in the lobby of Carter's apartment complex. Since she'd called her twenty minutes ago and told her what was going on, she'd been quiet. Eerily quiet, and not even Andrew seemed to be having any luck at bringing her out of it. When the pharmacy was surrounded, Murph walked over to her and pulled her chin around so that she had to look at her.

"You can do this. But if you can't, I can have my men go in and bring them out one at a time." Laci said that she had to do this. "I understand, but my men can handle this."

"I know that they can. But without them trying to kill me, you said they'd walk in a few hours. You needed more." Murph wished that she hadn't said that but couldn't take it back now. "I want them gone, from here and from my life. This is the only way. Besides, you said I'd be safe now. That even though they could hurt me, they couldn't kill me."

"You will be very safe. You're an immortal, but you can still get hurt." Laci nodded and looked at the elevator. Murph had sent one of her men up to the apartment where her aunt was being watched. "You did right by putting her to sleep. Had they gotten word on what we were doing, there's no telling what they might have done to the people inside."

"Killed them, you mean. Just as they had the people in the grocery store." Laci stood up, a look of hard determination on her face. "I'm going in now. The man behind the counter, he's with you? I mean, he's going to know what I'm doing."

"He does. The only people in the store as of right now are my men and the bad guys. Once you get in there, go

KATHI S. BARTON

straight to the counter and tell him what you're there for. An account set up in the name of Jeanie Wintermute." Laci said she understood, but Murph wanted to be sure. "When the shit hits the fan, you're to get behind the counter and stay there until I come for you."

"About my aunt. I need to know, Murph. She's going to go away, right?" Murph knew what Laci had been through in the last months and felt sorry for her. "She's tried to have me killed five times now, and that's attempted murder. So she's going to go to prison for a long time, right?"

"Yes. When this is done, myself and some other men are going to go up there and wake her. Then take her to jail. Once there, she'll have several chances to tell her side of the story. There are men coming from each place that you were set up to be killed. They'll want to talk to her about the deaths that she was a part of when things went sour." Murph looked at the building, then back at Laci. "They're not going to hurt you again, Laci."

"No, not physically they're not." Murph wanted to hug her to her. Laci was about the sweetest person she'd met, and this shit wasn't right. As she made her way to the building, one of her men going in at the same time, Murph looked at Andrew.

"She's going to be able to close this behind her when this is over, don't you think?" Andrew said he hoped so, but he wasn't sure. Murph nodded. It was her aunt after all. "My dad, he did a number on me. I still find myself, even after all this time, wondering what I did wrong to make him hate me so much."

"He was a prick and a bastard. To you and Max. I, for one, am glad that he's gone." She said she was as well. Murph looked at the building again and started toward it. Andrew called her name out and she turned back to him. "I

106

love you, Murph. You're the best sister a man could have. I just wanted you to know that."

She was nearly to the door when she heard the first shot. Hurrying now, she made her way into the building to see that Laci was out of sight, but her men were being shot at. Hoping the girl had done what she'd been told, Murph opened fire. Killing the first man she saw, Murph made her way to the counter where she hoped that Laci was.

Two of her men were down but not dead. Three of the guys that they'd been there for were down as well, one of them dead. As she made her way to the counter, she saw a man and nearly shot at him when he put his fingers to his lips. Murph was so shocked by the move that she stood there and watched as he went behind one of the shooters and snapped his neck and let him fall. Murph heard her name and looked to her right.

"Don't shoot him. He's helping us." Murph nodded at Laci and moved to stand where she was hiding. Not where she'd told her to go but close enough, Murph thought. "They were ready for you. I mean, almost as soon as I walked in the door, they were all over your men. I think they knew this was going to happen."

She watched the men from her position near Laci and could see that she might have been right. But when one of the men walked up behind her unknown helper, she shot him in the head. The man gave her a thumbs up as he moved on.

"Do you know him?" Laci said nothing, and she looked at her. "Laci, who is that man? Do you know him?"

"His name is Cyrus. I summoned him to me today when I felt his pain. I think that his other master hurt him and I could feel it." Murph wondered how the hell that had happened but before she could ask, Laci continued. "He was

107

hurt or I might not have helped him like I did. But it was that or have him die."

"You fed him." It wasn't a question, but Laci answered that she had anyway. "Do you have any idea what you did when you did that?"

"I saved his life, he told me. And he said that he owes me. I don't want him to owe me. To be honest, I think what he did for me with the envelope should have made us even." Murph had heard about that and had a new respect for the man. He moved in the direction of one of her men, and she nearly told him to back off when he broke his neck as well. Murph watched in stunned silence as he made his way to her. She never lowered her gun when he stood in front of her.

"They were aware of you coming here today. Each man has a mental picture of you and of young Laci here. That man, the one I killed for you, he was your leak." Murph asked him how he knew. "He is a friend of my maker. Or who I thought was my maker. I think there is something more to that as well, and I will find out, but for now, I am at your service. My name is Cyrus. You're Doran, I believe."

"I am." She glanced at Laci and she said she didn't say anything. Not that she knew what a Doran was to tell him. She looked back at Cyrus. "How did you know to come here? Or for that matter, how are you here in the daylight?"

"I think that her blood is that powerful." They both looked at Laci, who was red in the face. "She summoned me as well. I don't think that just anyone, especially not a human, as I was led to believe that she is, has done anything that kind for me in a very long time. I owe her my life, I think."

"None of us are what we let people believe we are." He nodded and bowed before standing again. "This master of yours, or whatever he might be to you, is he going to come looking for you? Do I need to bring in the troops?"

"I would say that is a good idea anyway. There are more men out there than this. Sonya has provided Martin with a seemingly endless supply of money and magic." Murph asked Cyrus what side he was going to be on when the storm came through. "I am wherever Laci needs me. Now and forever."

The building was brought to order by the men that had been on standby about an hour later. She'd only lost one man, and he was the man that Cyrus said was her leak. She thought perhaps he was right, too, when several hours later she noticed that his bank accounts had a huge influx of money over the last twenty-four hours. Plus, he had a stash of guns in his house and garage. Even his car had had enough guns and ammo in it to have taken the entire town out. Whatever he'd been up to, it hadn't been to help her department out.

And the deeper she dug into his life, the more she found out about Richard James. The little fucker was selling her out to a great many people, not just Martin and Sonya. He'd contacted newspapers, as well as a couple of labs that he thought might want a piece of her and her son.

So now she had to be on the lookout for men in white coats to come for her. It wouldn't be the first time, nor did she think it would be the last. But this time she didn't have the added mess that her father added to the equation. Murph let her son know what was going on and told him to be extra careful.

You as well. Kendra and I will be back in a few days. The hiking has been fun, but I think she's about done in with it. We have one more trip to make before our vacation is over. Then we're heading back for good. She told him how much she missed him.

109

And I do you too, Mom. Tell everyone to be safe and we'll see them on the flipside.

The baby took that moment to kick her, and she rubbed her hand over it to give her all her love. As soon as she was calm, Murph went to find her husband. She needed him and knew just where to find him.

CHAPTER 8

You might want to come to the cable office. Andrew rolled to his back and tried to think beyond the fuzzy exhaustion in his head. He asked Rider why he needed to go now. *Your office has been broken into, and your personal things have been destroyed. Also, and you're not going to believe this, the man responsible for it is sitting at your desk as we speak trying to clone your computer. When asked by the security team you have there, he said that you were told this would happen.*

Andrew sat up and reached for his pants. He hated to wake Laci, but as soon as he stood up she turned on the light and asked him where he was going. Andrew relayed to her what Rider was telling him.

"He's there with him?" Andrew said that he was watching him on the cameras they had in the offices. "And Blair is just waiting for you to come there and catch him?"

"I think he believes that he's in the right and that I shouldn't have done this to his office. He made it clear the other day when I was there that he was going to use my office regardless of what I did to keep him out." When he was dressed, she told him she was coming as well. "I think you should stay here, naked and waiting for me."

111

"I think you should stop thinking with your dick. I'm going." He left the bedroom when she told him to. Rider was giving him a blow by blow accounting of the actions of the man. So Andrew went to his office to wait for Laci and pulled up the cameras on his own computer.

What's he doing now? Rider laughed and told him. *So he's trying his best to get past the locking system I have in place and is pissed because of it.*

What I think he's mostly pissed about is that you've fixed the filing cabinets. I have to admit, I thought it was pretty smart of him to have the drawers all welded shut so you'd not be able to figure it out. But to have opened up the back of them, turning the files so that they were in the correct direction was brilliant. Andrew had thought so too when he'd been able to step back from it and think. *What's the plan? And so you know, I'm keeping a copy of this to show around to the family. This guy takes the cake.*

Blair had not only made it so the filing cabinets in his office were impossible to open, but he'd also made it so that if they were tampered with, there was a secondary locking system in place. If the code was put in improperly or not at all, the back of the cabinets would have a steel drawer come down over the files and lock. He'd almost locked himself out of the cabinets when the cabinet had been pulled from the wall. Lucky for him, his chair had been in the way and he'd only pulled it out a couple of inches. John had noticed the grooves before they'd done more damage to the stupid filing cabinets.

He watched the man for another ten minutes, waiting for Laci to come down. When she entered the office, he told Rider he was going in and to make sure that he kept an eye on him.

I will, but you make sure that he doesn't hurt either of you. There is something seriously wrong with that guy. And he talks to himself. Andrew pointed out that he did the same, and Rider laughed. *Yes, I do, but I don't answer myself. Nor do I have arguments. The really sad part is I don't think he wins many of them.*

Now that was insane. As they made their way over to the cable company, he asked Laci what she had planned for the day. He'd made arrangements with Rider and Carter to go junk hunting about a month ago, and she'd told him to go on and have fun. And Max had decided to go along with them, just for the fun of it.

"I'm going to go over to the antique store after this. They still don't have a name for it just yet. Max asked me to think about it, but I have no idea." Andrew told her she should give it some thought. "I will. But I have to see if I can do the job first. I know a lot about antiques, it was one of the many jobs that I had when I was still at home. And I can sell pretty much anything that is put before me, but I don't want to mess up. Max said that I'd do a good job and that'd be great for him. I think knowing something about the piece will be a lot more helpful."

"You'll be great at it." Laci leaned her head back on the seat as he continued. "We have a shipment coming in today. And Charlie is going to need some help with a big lot she has coming in today as well. Her building has finally been emptied out at where she was before and that stuff is being brought to her new place to work. I don't know what it is, but I'm assuming by what Misha was saying that it's a great deal of inventory that will need to be sorted and stored."

"Your mom said that her and Hannah were going to work for her. I think her baskets are beautiful. The one that she did up for Hannah and little Kelly was gorgeous. I could never think of something that put together. I'm more of a give me a plan and I can do it person than a person who just knows how things should be arranged."

"I've seen some of her things too. And I'm just as amazed. You should see her whip up a batch of soap. It's like watching a well-organized orchestra playing. And at the end, she has these little bars of the most wonderful smelling stuff." As they pulled into the parking lot, he turned to her. "You don't have to go in. I can handle him on my own. Why don't you go over to the shop? I know you have a key."

He could tell that she wanted to. Not so much to go to the shop but to not go in and confront Warren. Andrew was actually looking forward to it. Now that he had the list of names of the people that had been getting a portion of Laci's money, he was ready to confront the man on all levels. He saw Anderson, Carter's attorney, pulled in next to him. It was show time.

"Okay. I want to look around on my own anyway. I just want to make sure I'm doing the right thing." He knew that Laci was but didn't say it to her again. Instead he kissed her and watched her as she moved across the street to the building three blocks up from here. He knew that she'd be all right, but he still worried about her.

"You ready for this?" He grinned at Anderson when he spoke. "Yeah, you look every bit of the cat that you are right now. And I've been warned by Misha that I'm not to let you shift and kill the man. I haven't the slightest clue how he expects me to do that, but I told him I'd keep an eye on you."

"Thanks for coming out for me. I really appreciate it. Especially as late as it is." Anderson told him to wait for the bill. Even as they made their way to the door, Nic appeared beside them. "Christ, don't you have a warning light or something? I nearly pissed myself."

"You will need me around, I think." If Nic said you might need him, the likelihood that you did was high. "I have been looking into some things. And while this man has no idea who Sonya is, he has been in contact with Martin the vampire. Oh, and I have found out that Cyrus is not his child. That is the reason that Laci was able to call him to her."

They moved into the building and down the hall to his offices. There was only a few working this late at night. Most of them were even nodding off at their desks. The number of customers using this company over the larger one was small. Andrew had a feeling that by the end of the year he was going to have to close up. It just wasn't feasible for him to keep it running without much income. He was already making plans to turn it into something else anyway. Not what to use the building for, but just not a failing cable company.

Andrew stopped when they were about halfway down the hall. His door was gone. Not open, which was what he had expected, but gone. It lay on its side down the corridor from his office, and he noticed that the doorknob had been shot off. He moved into the room just as Warren was trying to get the cabinets to move from the walls.

"Those are stationary now. I think you will need more than a little help to get them away from the wall. Though why you would think you should is beyond me." Warren turned to him, his face screwed up in anger. "You were told to stay out of my office and off my computer."

"And I told you, several times as a matter of fact, that that doesn't work for me. I use this office and the computer when you are not here." Andrew crossed his arms over his chest and said nothing. "You have also tampered with my computer and the ones in these offices. I demand that you return them as they were. As well as these files. Were you not told to leave them alone? They are of no concern to you."

"They are because I said they were." Warren snorted at him and sat at his desk again. "You shot the door open. Why the hell did you do that? When, as I have mentioned several times now, you were not to be in my office."

"I also told you to give me a key. Why must you keep making this hard on me? I know what I'm doing and there is no reason for you to be barging in on my things making changes that have nothing to do with you." He looked at Anderson. "What is he doing here? I don't care for strangers in my building."

"It's my building and this is my attorney. Warren, I'm going to have to ask you for your badge. I haven't any idea how you got in anyway. I know for a fact that I disabled not only your badge but your sign-in as well." Warren didn't move. "Did you hear what I—?"

"Yes, yes, I heard you prattling on. You have no idea who you're messing with here, do you?" Andrew asked him to explain. "I run things the way I want them here. Not you. And the sooner you figure that out, the better things are going to be for you. As for how I got into *my* building, I got in here because the people who work here know who's in charge. They also know what will happen to them if they don't do as I say. You'll learn your place soon enough or you'll be gone as well."

"You go on thinking that. Where is Laci's money?" Warren said he had no idea who that was. "You knew her as Beth Summer. And she told me all about how you knew her real name. Where is the money she made in commissions for the last six months?"

"I would imagine that it's been spent. And if you want to know if I took it, then I'll tell you that I did. So what? She was a liar and had no rights to it anyway. The people I gave it to weren't making enough to make ends meet and I helped them out. She was still getting a part of it. I suppose she complained to you about it." Andrew told him that he'd discovered it on his own. "Oh well, good for you. But it's not like I took it all from her. What was she going to do with it anyway? It's not like she had a place to live where she had rent due like these people did."

"You do know that by taking her money you made it impossible for her to have a home or even enough food to eat. Not to mention that it was against the law, and that by doing so you will be brought up on charges." Warren said that wasn't his doing and he wasn't going to take the blame for her stupidity. "But you did take her money. Seven grand of it, as a matter of fact."

"The money went to a good cause. If she needed more, she should have worked harder for the rest of us." Andrew looked at Anderson when he laughed. "You should have seen her face when I told her what was going to happen. She learned her place fast enough. And as I said, it wasn't like the money was all going to me. Some of the people that I gave it to really needed it. Why, one of them was able to afford a new car with that money. I do wonder when she's coming back however. The money has sort of slowed since she's been gone."

"She won't be coming back here to work. She's my wife." Warren laughed. "You think it's funny that I married her?"

"No, I think it's funny that you thought you had to marry her. In my experience, women like her, they'll give it away for nearly nothing. Perhaps you should have cleared that with me before you said your vows. I could have saved you a great deal of money." The hand on Andrew's arm was the only thing that stopped him from leaping at the man. And when he continued spouting his free but useless advice, Andrew looked at Nic.

"He is not worth it. You know that, don't you?" Andrew nodded. "He's hanged himself now. The rest, as they say here, is gravy for the police. Young Murph has been listening in with your brother Rider. They are coming here now."

As soon as Murph walked in the door, Warren stood up. He was telling her about the things that Andrew had done to his office and to his computer while he was turned and cuffed. The complete look of shock on his face was evident when he realized that he was being arrested. Then Murph began reading him his rights.

"Shut your mouth right now. I am not going to stand for this. And you have no reason to arrest me. That man there, he's the one that messed with the natural order of things in my office. He should be put away forever. Get these things off of me this minute, you hear me?" Murph started reading him his rights again when he pulled away from her. "You cannot be seriously thinking I did anything wrong here. I am ruler here."

"Ruler? Well, okay then. Ruler Blair Warren, you're under arrest for breaking and entering, destruction of private property—" She was still reading off the list of shit he'd done today as they left his office, an officer on either side of him.

"Want my advice?" He told Anderson he would take anything he had to offer. "Close up. Sell what you can, but I'd not open my doors here again. Not as a cable company anyway. There is going to be bad blood here from now on. Even those that didn't care for Warren and his rules aren't going to be sticking around for much longer anyway. This place is dead, and they can see the writing on the wall even if you can't."

"I was thinking the same thing." Anderson told him he'd take care of it for him. "Not the building. I want it for another project. I have something in mind for it."

"I can help you with that as well."

After he left, Andrew sat at his desk. Even with all the stuff around him destroyed, he felt better about this than he had in a long time. Not just the business, but life in general.

~~~

Laci moved around the rooms. There was already a lot of furniture and other things in the lower levels that she thought could use a little polishing, and she was sure that there were things in the other darkened rooms that she'd not discovered as yet. The large case with the jewelry in it was simply too pretty to resist.

"I can open it for you if you'd like." Laci screamed when Max spoke to her. "I'm sorry. I should have warned you that I was here. I forget sometimes that you can't feel me around like the others. It's because we've not touched."

"And I don't think we will either, thanks. I've had enough magic zapped on me for a lifetime or two." He said nothing but moved to the other side of the glass case from her. "I've never seen such beautiful things before. Andrew said you got most of it from estate sales and such."

"I did. Mom and I would go to them when we could. Not often, but we'd sneak out. It was fun. And I began collecting things that I liked then and stashing them away here and there. It's amazing what you can do when you have enough power behind you to hide it." She just nodded. To her, Max was freaky scary in what he could do. He was also a very nice young man, and she was glad to have him on her side. When he laughed, she told him she was sorry. "No worries. I'm sorry I intruded on your thoughts. When Mom and I are at the house with Dad, we have a rule. No looking until you think it's necessary. You do know that you can do it too, don't you?"

"I'm not sure I'm ready for all that as yet." He nodded again and unlocked the big case. "Can I see the blue piece, the bracelet? The one with the large pearl in the center. I think that's the prettiest piece in here."

"Believe it or not, I got this at an auction and paid a whole dollar for the entire box of jewelry. I had no idea it was even in the box until I got it home and started separating things out. I like it too." He handed it to her and Laci had a moment of panic. Something touched her skin. "Are you all right?"

"Yes." But the feeling wasn't going away. In fact, she felt as if she were being grabbed by something bigger than her. And meaner. "The woman who owned this was being abused, I think. The man hurting her, he's calling her names and telling her that he's going to be rid of her in a fortnight."

"Can you see him?" Laci felt herself turn, and she looked at the man standing just behind her. But she thought she was seeing things wrong and told Max that. "It's all right. Just tell me what he looks like. You can see the violence of the piece. Not just the woman. Tell me what he's saying to her. What he has on. What he looks like."

"Taller than her by about a foot. He has dark hair. Red I think. His face is scarred. He has a long cut above his brow and the scar runs deep in his cheek." Laci wanted to drop the bracelet, but Max told her to hold it and tell her what else she saw. "He has on a gold chain. Thicker than my fingers, and there is a large diamond in the center of it. He has on velvet and lace. It's sticking out of his jacket like he wants to show it off."

"He more than likely did. Can you see any of the room? Perhaps something hanging on the wall?" She looked again but was slapped. Or the woman had been. There wasn't any pain for her, but she felt it, as if it were a memory rather than an actual hitting. "Laci, it's not real, what you're seeing. It's only the things that the woman saw and felt when she was wearing it."

"A crown, he has it on a statue near a bed. The bed is old, draped in lace and sheer stuff. Silk, I think and it's blue...maybe purple." Laci had a thought when she realized what he'd said to her. "Max, this is real, isn't it? I'm really seeing what she did."

"Yes. I'm sure of it. You can touch things and bring their wearer to life. I wonder if you can do that with furniture as well." She put the bracelet back and stepped away from the case. "You weren't hurt. And what you did was learn something great about the piece. It's like you're a walking history book for the things here."

"I don't think I want to know some of the things that went on with this stuff." He nodded and put the bracelet away. "I think he was going to kill her."

"He more than likely did." She nodded and looked around the store with new eyes. "Laci, don't let this frighten you. What you know about things will make you a better sales person. People, as you know, like a good story. And you'll have the best ones."

"Because I know that the woman who wore this was more than likely killed by her lover or husband?" He told her that she could change that to suit her needs. But the timeframe, the period in which it was first used, would lend so much to the way people would view things. "So I'm to skip over the murder part and say that it was from the twelfth century?"

"The fourteenth if your description is anything to go by." She frowned at him when he laughed. "You are going to have such fun here."

"How can you —?"

The knock at the door startled them both. And when he pushed her behind him, Laci had a moment of fear. But the woman standing at the door looked drenched. Her hair was in strings around her face and shoulders.

"I thought it was you." Before she could ask Max what he meant, he moved toward the door and unlocked it. That was when she realized that it wasn't a woman as she'd thought, but a man. With long golden hair. And he had the most calming smile she'd ever seen on anyone before.

"I saw your lights and thought I'd come see if I could get warm. My car broke down some miles back." Max stared at the man without answering him, so Laci moved forward. "I mean no harm to you. I just wanted to get warm."

"I'm Laci. This is my nephew Max." The man didn't offer his hand, and she didn't either. "We were just going over some of the inventory. You were lucky to catch us. My husband is on his way over."

"I'm Tristin." He looked around. "This is a beautiful place you have here. I guess you're not open yet, are you?"

"In a few weeks." Laci was sort of worried about Max. He'd said nothing nor moved since he'd let the man in. "Let me get you a towel. I saw some in the back room when I was looking around."

She didn't want to leave Max with the man, but she figured that if anyone could handle the man he could. According to Murph, he was the strongest being alive. When she returned, Max looked as if he'd gotten his tongue back and was talking to Tristin. Laci reached out for Andrew and let him know what was going on.

Max is surprised about something? Gosh, let me come right over and take a video of him. That's a first as far as I can remember. She laughed. *I'll be over soon. If you're okay. I just need to go over some of the stuff here. Then I'm closing up.*

I'm so sorry. You really wanted it to work. He told her that he was sort of relieved not to have to worry about it anymore. *Then good. I'll work for us both. How much is our house payment, so I know how much money to ask for from Max when he starts paying me?*

Honey, you just have fun. We have more than enough money for whatever we want to do. Trust me. She found that she did. More than she could have ever imagined she would another person. She was still talking to Tristin and Max when Kendra showed up.

CHAPTER 9

Kendra found herself at a loss for words. The man standing with her friend was beautiful, and she found that she wanted not just to touch him but to wrap herself around him. But when he turned his back to her, talking to Laci instead of her, all she could think about was that she wanted to harm him. Reaching out her hand to jerk him back to her and slap him, Max was suddenly in front of her.

"What are you doing?" She didn't have any idea and backed from him. "Do you feel it, Kendra? Can you tell what he is to you?"

"I have no idea what you mean. He turned his back on me." Max nodded and watched her. "No one does that to me. I am queen."

"You are, but why would he know that?" She thought that he should simply know. He was genjar after all. "You're being unreasonable. You know that, don't you? Why is that, you think?"

Her anger was out of control. She knew this. Kendra wanted to blame it on the man, but Max was right. He had no idea who she was. Her face might be on the coin that they used as well as money, but he had no reason to think she was the one and same woman. Instead of pointing out that she was as confused as she'd ever been, she decided to just go back to their campsite.

"I'll be there when you return. I had thought you'd be back by now. When you said you wished to check on Laci, I knew you'd return soon. Then an hour passed, and I got worried." He just stared at her. But the man continued to ignore her and it bothered her a great deal. "Who is this person, and why is he here?"

"He said he was only getting in out of the rain. I don't know anything else about him yet." Kendra realized she was rubbing her hands together. She wanted to touch the man but was afraid to. He was still not looking at her, but that mattered little to her right now. "Kendra, are you going back now?"

"Yes. Now." Still, she stood there, staring at the strange man as if she'd never seen one before. He was so handsome. He was tall, taller than her by a good four inches. His arms were muscled. Even his neck was thick with them. And his body looked sculpted from stone. Like the castle where she lived, hard and unyielding. "I'm not sure where he came from. I'm not sure that I like how he just showed up either."

"I don't know either, but it's fine if you want to go back." She nodded at Max again, trying her best to think what was wrong with her. The man turned to them, and she had a feeling that he could hear her heart pounding in her chest. Because it was—hard and fast—and she wasn't sure why. "Kendra, are you all right?"

"Yes. Of course...no. I don't know what's wrong all of a sudden. Do you suppose I caught something when we were playing in the water at the campsite?" Max said he doubted it. "I need to touch him." Max laughed then left her alone with the man.

The man continued to stare at her, his eyes burning into her as if he were looking deeper into her than anyone had before. She felt her mouth dry and her tongue thicken in her mouth. Even her breasts felt heavy with some unknown force. The need to feel them in his mouth embarrassed her. When he took a step toward her, she took one back.

"I'm the queen. You don't touch me unless I say you can." He just grinned at her, and she took another step back when he took two toward her. "I command that you stop where you are. You're not to come any closer to me."

"I need to see if you're real." She told him she was as real as him. "Are you? My name is Tristin by the way. And I have never seen such beauty before. Words fail me in trying to think just how to tell you how lovely you are. But I've a feeling that you know that. That you're as aware of your beauty as I am."

"You make me sound conceited. I'm not. You need to stop that. Right now." The wall behind her touched her back. Before she could move away, Tristin had her blocked by his hands on either side of her body. "You're making me afraid."

"No I'm not. You're far from afraid of me." She put her hand out to shove him away, but he captured it in his own hand. "You're who I've been looking for my entire life. I can't believe I found you now. I have you now and I'm never letting you go, Kendra, Queen of the Genjar."

"I don't know what you're talking about. I want you to leave me alone. I have no time for such foolishness. I am the ruler of my kingdom and you are nothing to me." He pressed his body into hers and she felt his length, his muscles, and his cock as he rocked into her. "I don't want you to do that."

"Yes you do. You want me to do more." Her body was telling her to let him while her mind was still trying to get him to understand that she was a queen. "Kendra, I'm going to kiss you now. Then when I finish, I want you to tell me that I mean nothing to you. That you wish for me to leave you alone."

"I'll tell you that now. I'm Queen Kendra to you. Or Lady Kendra. You will not address me so personally." He moved again, his cock seemingly thicker, harder as he lifted her ass up to meet each thrust. "You're going to make me come."

"I should hope we both can." His mouth was taking her. It wasn't a kiss but a taking and she knew this. And when his tongue moved along hers, dueling with it as one would with a sword, she put her hands on his shoulders to hold on. Kendra knew as surely as she was standing there that if she did come, which was highly likely, she was going to come apart into pieces. When he lifted his mouth from hers, she whimpered. "When we come together, Lady Queen, I will rule the bed. If you wish to rule the kingdom with me at your side, then so be it. But in the bed...."

He lifted her up higher, and she had no choice but to wrap her legs around him. She willed them to her home, to her bed, and he laid her over it as he took her throat, her mouth, and even her breast into his mouth. He suckled at her nipple and her flesh beneath her breast. As he made his way down her ribs, biting and kissing her as he went, all she could think about was having him inside of her. His body one with hers.

When he stood up, his body as naked as hers was now, she touched her finger to his cock, the tip soaked in his cream. He told her to take it to her mouth, and she nearly fainted at the taste of him. Before she could beg him for more he was on his knees in front of her, her thighs on either side of his head.

"I'm going to drink of you. Then I'm going to take you as mine. Say it, Kendra, say that you belong to me." She shook her head, and his hand smacked across her thigh. "Say you belong to me and none other, Kendra, and I will make you mine."

"I am ruler of this kingdom." It sounded lame even to her. "Please, Tristin. I need something from you. Please?"

He suckled her clit into his mouth, and she came up off the bed. There was no relief for her, only more need when he continued to tease and play with her. Just as she was ready to release, he would pull back, beg her again to say it, and she would refuse each time. Finally, when he slid his finger into her pussy, she knew that he wasn't going to give her what she wanted until she gave him his due.

"I belong to you and none other." He nipped at her clit and a small climax took her breath away. "More. I beg of you, more."

"I need it all. Tell me, Kendra, tell me that you are my mate, tell me that you will belong only to me." Her body was on fire. Even the slightest breath over her pussy had her sobbing with need. "Say it and I will end this for you."

"I am your mate, now and forever. I will give you all that I am, hold nothing back from you as my lover. You will rule with me, beside me for the rest of my days, father my children and love them as I do." He told her to say it all, there was more. She knew it as well; the pledge of marriage had been something she'd known since birth. "I will love you with all that I am. Keep you safe, seek your counsel above all others. You will have my heart, my love, and none other will ever come between us. I, Kendra, First Queen to the Eighth House of Elders, give you, Tristin, king to my queen, all that I have and more."

He entered her then, his cock filled her in places that had nothing to do with her body. Her mind was filled with his, memories as his merged with hers. His heart beat with hers, and his blood would forever pulse throughout both their bodies for all time. And when he pulled her body to his, fucking her as hard as he could, Kendra pulled his throat to her mouth and sealed the bond between them as she came hard. Taking his blood into her body and giving him hers would mate them for all eternity. She cried out when he gave her all that he was in return.

Kendra felt the moment that the kingdom became aware of him. Knew the exact moment that her family knew that she'd found her mate and that they were one. Letting the darkness slide over her, Kendra wondered what she was supposed to do now. She'd taken her mate.

He was holding her when she woke. His body, much harder and larger than hers, was comforting. The blanket over them made her realize that he'd seen to their needs before he'd taken a rest. When he kissed her shoulder, she wanted to feel embarrassed but snuggled closer to him.

"You're my mate. You understand that, don't you?" She nodded, unsure what to say to him now. "Kendra, are you going to be upset when we leave this room?"

"Probably." One thing she knew about mates, there was no lying to them. If a question was asked, then you had better be prepared for the answer. "I don't know what to do with you. I rule and you cannot interfere."

"You think I'll interfere with your work?" Tristian rolled her to her back, and he loomed over her. "You and I have a lot of things to talk about, and the first thing is that I don't consider helping my mate as interfering."

Kendra got out of the bed, completely forgetting that she was naked. And when he stood up as well, it was all she could do not to stare at him. Christ, the man was beautiful. Instead of arguing with him more, not that she could remember what it had been about, she watched him as he fisted his cock over and over.

"Come here." She found herself moving toward him even as her mind was telling her no. "I'm going to tell you this again. And this time you will listen to me. I am your mate. But here in this room or wherever I take you, I rule you. Understand? Say it for me."

"I need to rule." He wrapped her hand around his cock, and she moaned. "Take me again, Tristin. I want to come with you inside of me."

"I rule your body. Say it, Kendra. When we're alone, I am the master of your body." She felt the thick cream leak from the tip and wanted to take it and him into her mouth, but he jerked her head up when she bent to taste him. "You want me then you know who rules the bedroom. Say it and I'll fuck you hard enough that you see stars."

"I hate you." He laughed as he slid his fingers into her pussy. She tried to ride him, bring herself to peak, but again he only teased her until she wanted to hurt him. "I'm to rule the kingdom, but you rule this bedroom."

"Nay, I will take you in more places than this room alone. I want your body to be mine. So when I wish to fuck you, you'll do as you're told." She felt her pussy gush cream at the thought of him taking her in the throne room, in her bath, and even out of doors. "Say it and I'll take you in all of those places and more."

"You rule my body. Now fuck me." He laughed and turned her around. Before she could understand his intent, he pulled her across his lap when he sat on the side of the bed. When his hand came down hard on her bottom, she struggled to get away, but he only spanked her harder.

Kendra came twice before he flipped her to the bed and fucked her again.

~~~

Linyah watched her sister. If she wasn't so worried about her, she might have thought it funny. When she made her way to where she was sitting, Linyah waited for her to speak first. When she didn't, she asked her how it was going.

"He thinks to rule me." Linyah felt her protectiveness for her sister flare up. "And I asked Max. To see if he brought him to me, to make me have a mate, but he says that he did not. I don't want someone manipulating my life around where they think I need a mate. I don't. And I told him that. But I don't know about him ruling my body either. He wishes it to be my body where he rules me and not just the bedroom. Not as a ruler but in the...you know. Then what is to say he won't make me do things I don't want?"

Linyah looked at Tristin, then back at her sister. He was watching her, in much the same way that Thomas watched her. Hungry and sort of sappy. When it occurred to her what Kendra was talking about, Linyah decided to have some fun with her.

"I doubt very much that he wants to rule the kingdom. And I don't really understand what you mean by ruling you elsewhere. You just said that he doesn't want to make himself the ruler of our lands. I would have thought that you'd put your foot down on that. Women have been the rulers here since—"

"Not that. He doesn't have any problem with me ruling. He means with sex." Kendra's face flared to a deep crimson. "And he thinks that the bedroom isn't the only place he should rule my body either. He said that we'd have it everywhere. I don't think that's such a good idea."

"Why not? Thomas and I go outside and make love. Sometimes in the car. Once we even did it in your throne room." Kendra looked at her so shocked that Linyah laughed. "Don't be such a prude. Is sex that bad with him?"

"No." She seemed to realize that she'd been loud and let out a long breath before continuing. "No, it's wonderful. And he is very good at making me enjoy it as well."

"Then what's the problem? Does he hurt you?" Kendra's face got red again. "Kendra, does he like it rough? And you don't?"

"He spanks me. Hard, but I like it. No, that's not right. I love it. But it's not seemly, is it? To have a man spank you like a small child? Then there are the other things. He tied me to the bed too. I thought perhaps he was going to murder me, and I was so terrified. Then he started to touch me and do things to me that he was...I shouldn't be telling you this." Linyah asked her why not. "Because it's a private thing. And I don't want you to dislike him."

"I don't. Especially since he's got you all tied up in a knot." Kendra smiled, then looked at her with a frown. "Now what is it? He's not making you do things you don't want, is he? Are you afraid of him doing the things he does to you?"

"No. But some of them are...strangely sexy." Linyah laughed and Kendra smiled again. "You must think me silly. Like a small school girl with her first experience with men. It is, but I've been around men my whole life. I should be used to them and their ways."

"Why? All men are not alike. Some of them like things to be their way. Others are fine with going along with the person who knows the best way to make it work." She looked over at her own mate. "Thomas knows more about being around humans and their ways than anyone I know.

Especially me. But I know security and the elements that go with it, so that part he leaves up to me. Not that I don't listen when he suggests something, but we work together and that's what a good solid relationship is about."

"But I'm ruler and he doesn't seem to care." Linyah asked her sister why he should care. "Because I don't want him to forget that I rule. It's the only thing I have to offer anyone."

"Oh Kendra, I don't think he cares if you rule or not. And you have a great deal to offer him and anyone else if they want to look deep enough. He's in love with you. He wouldn't care if you were a dung mistress, shoveling out stalls for the rest of your life, so long as you can be together. Why do you need for him to realize that you rule? Are you afraid that he'll try and take over?" She said she wasn't. "Then why keep harping on that?"

"Because I'm not like you." Linyah felt the pain of her words to her heart. "I mean, you're so secure in your life and the one you have with Thomas. I don't know what I'm doing. You know everything."

Linyah laughed and Kendra started to walk away, but she stopped her. "Do you think it comes easily to me? Having a mate that is as different to me as anything in the world? At least Tristin is like us. He understands the ways of our kind. He knows what you're capable of and how you are the ruler of the lands. Don't push him away because you don't understand. Talk to him."

"I don't know what to say to him that will not make me sound like a fool." Linyah watched Tristin come toward them. "He might hate me when he finds out I've not a clue what I'm doing."

"He won't. I promise you." When Tristin wrapped his arms around Kendra, her sister seemed to melt against him.

It was the way it should be, each of them offering the other comfort when they needed it. Linyah reached out to her sister and told her what she had before. To talk to her mate and tell him her fears. *He will never hate you, Kendra. He is in love with you.*

When they left the room, just faded out, Linyah wondered what sort of adventure they would get into now. Smiling, she looked at her mom when she sat beside her. She seemed to be glowing with happiness.

"She's all right, isn't she?" Linyah told her she thought that her sister was very all right. "I so worried about her. A few weeks ago, when she and Max started out on their adventure, she told your father and me that she was going to find a mate that she would be able to rule. And basically stick in a corner until she was ready for him to come out and hang on her arm. I had hoped that she'd find something very unlike that."

"She has." Her mom looked at her. "He's not going to rule her, at least not outside of sex. But she worries that he won't let her be in charge. I think that will come to her after a while. She's insecure, she told me, too."

"She is. I've noticed that all my children are to a point. Even you." Linyah knew that she had been. Even now she was still insecure in her actions, especially around Thomas. But she also knew that she was getting stronger all the time. "He's a nice person, her Tristin. I think he will do well beside her. But I doubt he'll stay in the corner for long. Do you?"

"No. He won't. But I don't think he'll rule either. He knows what is needed of him." Her mom sat there, just looking around the room. Linyah did as well. They were a very eclectic family, she thought. Her mom spoke again before she could put too much thought into it.

"Do you ever stop to think how this all came about? The families, I mean." She told her mom she was just thinking about how they were all so different. "Not so much really. Men and women really. But what I meant was, the way we all connected. Had Hannah really died when Sonya had said, none of this would have come to pass. Hannah brought us Misha in her own way. Then with Misha having Thomas as a brother, he became a part of our family in a large way. Nic watched over Murph for Carter or she'd not be here either, bringing us her son. Then there is Max and the Dorans. We have a larger family now, thanks to his having a grandmother that worships him. A larger force too...I think Sonya found that out the hard way. Andrew brought us, in a way, Tristin and a love for our Kendra by falling in love with a woman that has some special abilities which brought her to the antique store that night."

"There is also Charlie and Phillip. Had he not taken her as his mate and brought her here to save her, she too would have died and left a hole in all of our hearts. Now she is a happy, healthy woman, something that I think she's not been for a long while." They both looked at Rider, the last Lanning to be single. So far. "His mate won't be like the others. Not entirely anyway. She'll be magical, strong, with all the elements in both realms. Happy, but only after Rider finds her and brings her to his heart. Our mates do that for us. Even I wasn't as strong as I wanted until I met Thomas."

"I think Rider's mate, when she comes, will be the strongest of them all. Mostly due to what you've done to him. He still has no idea what it is, does he?" Linyah told her he didn't. "Taking him the way that you did, holding him safe for what will come to him, you did him a great service. I wonder if he will ever know the sacrifice you made to claim him."

"It wasn't a sacrifice to me. I liked him even then. And had I not, then we both know what would have happened to him in the future." Her mom nodded sadly. "He belongs to me, and whoever comes to take him, and they will, Rider will not be beheaded, nor will he die at the hands of someone stronger than any of us. I told you this."

"Yes, you did. And I have seen it too, the future he has now over the one that he would have had. The woman is still a blur, but the man, he is there. I see him every time I close my eyes." Linyah shivered. She saw him as well. Thomas wasn't aware that the man who would have killed his brother lurked close by, even now. "You will tell him, will you not? Someday, you'll give him what he needs to break the bond between the two of you?"

"I will. But only to give it to his mate. She will hold him then, as it should be." Linyah couldn't see her, but she knew that she was stronger than any of them. Both in personality as well as magic. "Max cannot see her either. I've asked him what he knows of Rider's mate. He thinks he cannot because of the bond I have with him. I hope that holds true to the one that comes for him."

"As do I. I think…I have no idea why, but I think when the time comes we will need all our strength to keep us whole." Linyah said nothing to her mom. Whatever was coming for Rider, it was going to be quite the war. "You will keep them safe, won't you, love? All of us, you'll keep us as safe as you can?"

"I will die to protect what is mine." Her mom thanked her and moved away. Linyah watched her family and knew that what she had said to her mom was true. She would gladly die for any of them.

CHAPTER 10

Andrew held up the small lamp and thought it was the ugliest thing he'd ever seen. To think that this person wanted an entire dime for it; he thought them asking too much. Maybe they should have given a dime to someone who would take it from them. Sitting it back down on the table, he looked at Max.

The kid was having a great time, and a very profitable one. He'd purchased a dresser for his shop, a box of jewelry, as well as several boxes of old clothing. The rest he could understand, but the clothing he didn't. Andrew was planning to ask him about it as soon as they got back to their hotel.

Carter had backed out at the last minute. Not that he wanted to, but he'd heard about a tag sale in the opposite direction they were headed and he went with Rider. Andrew wondered if that trip was as fun as the one he and Max were on. They'd been gone three days so far, and had had to ship things home twice. Not the furniture, but some of the smaller items.

"You should buy that." He looked at Max, then at the lamp he'd only just sat down. "There are enough parts on it that you can make your money back in no time."

"It's ugly." Max laughed. "Why would anyone save something like this for years and years? Seriously. I might have accidently broken it when it was given to me." He glanced around the garage they were in and noticed something he'd not seen before. "Did you see that trunk over there?"

"No. I didn't. Darn it. You want it now, don't you?" Andrew did but not to sell. There was something about it that he loved, even at first glance. "Go see if it's for sale. I've not had much luck on the other items they have around. Why would one put out things and then say that they've decided not to sell?"

"I have no idea. Remember that woman in the other house? She nearly had a fit when I asked her if she'd go any lower on the box of door knobs. I thought that seven thousand dollars was way too much for nine door knobs." Max laughed with him as they made their way to the truck. "It doesn't have a price tag on it."

It was gorgeous. Leather straps and brass fittings. There was a skeleton key hanging from the lock that turned easily enough. It had been well cared for, that much was obvious. When he opened it, he nearly slammed it shut again, not wanting anyone to see the treasures inside. He looked at Max when he decided that he'd pay anything they wanted for the trunk so long as he could have it all.

"You like that?" The woman that had been sitting behind her makeshift desk smiled at him. "It was my grandfather's and he loved it very much. I just don't care for old things like he did. That's what most of these things are. His. We put him in a nursing home about three months ago, and I just don't want to store this in my basement anymore. He was a collector, he said. I called him a hoarder. I love him so very much, but he had more stuff than we could fill four houses with."

Andrew nodded that most everything in her garage was older than he was. But he really did want this chest. And its contents. Smiling, he looked at the woman again.

"It doesn't seem to have a price on it. And I was wondering if it came the way it is. I noticed that there were some things still inside." She was nodding even before he finished. "Is it for sale then?"

"Oh yes, it goes like it is. I didn't think anyone would want that old stuff either, and hoped to kill two birds with one stone." She looked around the thing. "I swear it had a price sticker on it. Oh well, how about five bucks? It's really too heavy for me to carry back to the basement."

He looked at it then, trying his best not to look excited. Five bucks? Sure, he'd pay that. Andrew had been willing to pay five hundred for it. When she lowered her price down to two dollars, he told her he'd take it off her hands.

After paying her for it, he took it out to the trailer that they'd rented to do this trip with. The lock was cheap looking, but they'd had a little magic put on it before leaving and now he was glad that they had. As he was locking up, a man spoke behind him.

"I was gonna buy that." Andrew said nothing to the older man. "You have to go back and tell her you changed your mind. I really do want that. For my granddaughter's bedroom. She was gonna put her dollies in it and their things. I need that chest for my granddaughter, and you need to sell it back to her so I can get it."

"I'm sorry. But I've already paid her." He nodded but told him he really did want it. "So do I. And as I said, I've paid her for it. I'm sorry."

"No, I don't think you understand. I want you to take that out of there and hand it over. I need that chest for my granddaughter. She has had her eye on it since they brought it home from that old man's house." He smiled at Andrew, and he felt his skin crawl. "Now, I'm trying really hard to be nice here."

"No you're not. You're rude. And as I have said, several times, I'm not selling it or giving it back. I have it now and that's where it's going to stay." The man took a swing at him, and Andrew only ducked. He didn't fight back. There was no need to. The man fell on the ground and lay there looking up at him. "What is wrong with you? It's just a trunk that I now own."

"It's mine, I tell you. I want it now." When he started back up off the ground, the woman who had sold him the trunk put her foot on his chest. "Martha, I told you I wanted that trunk. You should have sold it to me, not this upstart. I told you several times that I was gonna pay you fair and square for it, and you went and sold it out from under me."

"He paid me, when all you did was make promises that you would. He paid me, as you said fair and square, and you lost out. Now go home before I call your missus." The man grumbled but got up to leave. When he entered the house across the street, Andrew thanked her. "No problem. Harvey is harmless really. He's been telling me for weeks now that he wanted the chest for his granddaughter. He doesn't have one. Not any children at all. Two weeks ago he came here telling me to sell him my dog. I don't have one of those either. But he had it in his head that he wanted me to sell him to him and finally I had to call his wife. Poor old thing gets confused."

Andrew thanked her again and went back to find Max. He wanted to leave, but Max had found something that he wanted and Andrew watched him while he spoke to Laci.

I just bought a trunk for the house. It's beautiful and well cared for. And inside of it are the most wonderful things. She asked him what. *Hats. Men's and women's hats from the twenties and thirties, I think.*

Hats? Old hats? I love hats. He knew this. She'd told him the other day how she'd collected them when she'd had the money, but had lost them all when she and her aunt had run. Andrew had someone packing up her house now and was having her things brought to her as a surprise. *I don't suppose there are any with veils, are there? I so love those.*

I didn't get too look that closely, but I could see a pale yellow one with what appeared to be a veil on it. I'm not going to go through it all until I can do so with you. He felt her love. *I love you as well. How is the shop going? Have you gotten our latest shipment?*

It came this morning. Charlie came over to help me when your note said that there were things in there for her. She loves the tiny baskets. I think she's going to make some ornaments out of them. Charlie is so creative. She was at that and he agreed with her. *Oh, and the soap molds that you found too, she's going to start making some of those on her next batch. I had no idea that those things were even around anymore. I thought that they would have been melted down for scrap. She acted like you'd given her the keys to the castle when she opened the case up.*

Max has some old jewelry too he's sending home to you. And you should expect a couple more boxes. Clothing in one, and the other is just odds and ends of things we've found. She told him she'd watch for it. *I love you, Laci. I don't think I tell you that nearly enough.*

And I love you as well. When do you think you guys will be back? And Carter called, he said that he's rented a large moving truck. He's made a hell of a deal on some household things. I'm almost afraid to see. He laughed when she did. *I miss you.*

I miss you as well. We've about six more stops to make today, then we'll go back to the hotel. I can meet you there, at the house, in about two hours if you want. Or in the back room of your shop? I need you. Andrew had been going home at night after Max had fallen asleep. It had been a wonderful time, making love to his wife and then going out all day with young Max. *I think he knows, by the way, that I'm leaving him at night.*

I'm sure that he does. He might be young, but he's not stupid. She laughed, and he asked her what was going on. *Max told me before you guys left that I could clean out the back room for him. There is all kinds of junk in there, and I thought it would make a good cleaning room. You know, someplace to polish up the things brought in here rather than on the floor. Anyway, I'm finding the strangest things. I found an old ledger. It has listed what someone had been storing. But it doesn't say where it might be.*

I'm sure if you just put it aside, whatever it is, it'll turn up later. She said she had an entire box of things like that. *I love you.*

I love you too.

Closing down the connection, he went to find Max. When he said he was ready to go, the two of them made their way back to the van and moved to the next home. He thought that they were going to either have to find a shipping company soon or they were going to quit. He was actually ready for the latter of the two.

"One more street, then we can go." Andrew asked him if he'd had enough or thought he did. "I've had enough. And I miss my bed. I'm having fun, but I'm ready to go home."

"Yeah, me too." Pulling up in front of the next string of houses that they were going to visit, he looked over at the younger man. "I'm really glad that we did this. You're a lot of fun."

"Thanks. You're not so bad yourself."

~~~

Monroe looked at the thing in front of him. It was a person, yes, but not much of one now. He'd had too much fun, he supposed, or he'd let his anger get the better of him. Smiling, he thought that his temper hadn't been this unleashed in a great many years. It had felt good, too good he supposed, to let it out for a little while. But he wasn't finished just yet. Martin still had information that Monroe needed. Or really, he just wanted it.

"You never answered me when I asked you why you thought to take my child. I should like your version of what transpired. Because, you see, you led people to think that he was yours, and we both know that is not the case. Cyrus was mine." Monroe thought of Cyrus, all these years he'd been lost to him. Something had kept him from finding the one man that he'd grown to cherish above all others. A friend. "Tell me, Martin. My time with you is growing boring."

"He was lost. And I found him. For all these years, I cared for him as my own. You should ask him about it. He was lost, I tell you." Someone, some magical creature, had hurt his Cyrus, and his mind had been blocked from him. It was the only explanation that he could think of. Monroe had been injured and had gone to ground for a time. And when he arose, his child was lost to him. Not dead, but lost. "I found him wandering the streets, and he came to me willingly."

A kick to the head rendered the man unconscious. Standing up and pacing, Monroe thought about just destroying the man, then going to find Cyrus. He knew only that he lived and that he had been under this man's power, but nothing more. Reaching out again, he hit the same wall, but this time he felt a woman instead of a male answer his call.

Who is this? She didn't speak, but he knew that she could hear him. *When I ask a question, I demand an answer. I am not one to trifle with. Who is this? I shall not ask you —*

You didn't ask at all, you overbearing shit. You demanded. And I don't respond well to dick heads. You want a question answered by me, then you fucking well better be polite about it. He wanted to be angered by her words, but instead he found himself admiring her. He was still going to hurt her, but he did like that she stood up to him. *Now, we're going to start over. If you want something, ask. You don't have to scream questions at me.*

Her voice was soft, kind. Monroe found himself leaning against the wall to relax his anger and to continue speaking with her. Like a game of chess, he knew for some reason that she'd give him his due and not let him win because he was who he was. Smiling, he answered her.

I'm sorry. He found that he was. *I'm only asking because I was looking for a dear friend of mine and I connected with you. A female. I was angry already, but I should not have taken it out on you.*

He felt...well, strangely attracted to her when she told him it was all right. Not in a sexual way...for all he knew she could be several decades old and have no teeth. But he didn't think so. He thought her to be young and smart. Very smart.

I don't know who you might be looking for. I'm fairly new to this mind connecting thing. I don't even know if you can get wires crossed or sort of dial up the wrong number when you reach out to people. Maybe if you tell him his name, I can tell you if I know him. He told her, knowing that there was something crossed somewhere and he was somewhat sad to lose the connection to her. *The vampire, Cyrus?*

His body stiffened at her question. Yes, he wanted to scream at her, then demand that she tell him where he was. But he also knew that should he try anything so stupid as to do that, she'd close him down and hide his friend from him. But his excitement won out over his caution.

You know him? Where is he? Is he well? Where can I find him? Tell me now. There was silence at the other end. *I'm sorry again. I have searched for him for many years, and I thought at one point him dead. Now I know someone that knows his whereabouts and I'm excited. You have no idea how hard I have searched. I miss him like I would my hand or my heart.*

You're not his maker. Or at least that's what Cyrus told us. This other jerk is. And so you know, I'm going to kick his ass when I find him too. I'm going to summon him to me and kick the ever loving shit out of him. He started to ask her how the hell she was going to do that when she spoke again. *He was hurting Cyrus, and I called him to me to save him. Cyrus was good to me when he wasn't supposed to be, and I could feel his pain.*

That's not possible. You cannot summon a vampire to you unless he's yours. She told him that she had and that she would again. *Where are you now? I should like to see Cyrus and talk to him.*

No. I don't think so. He started to tell her he damned well would when she spoke again. *For all I know you could be with that other shit, Martin whatever. Did you know that he's trying to kill me? All because some chick told him to. Well, guess what? You and that guy can kiss my ass. You are not going to hurt me, and Cyrus is going to be safe. I'm going to make sure of it.*

He loved this woman. Monroe had no idea why, but he had just fallen in love with her and her inability to be anything but respectful of him. She was feisty and full of indignation. Protective of things that were more than likely much stronger than her, and she was watching over his Cyrus. But he still was confused as to how she'd called Cyrus to her. He would find out, but now he only wanted to see his child.

My name is Monroe. I am his maker. If you would be so kind as to ask him about me, I know that he'd remember. Tell him...tell him that I miss him and his books. I have them still. She was quiet again, and he wondered if Cyrus was there with her. *Please, I would very much be indebted to you should you do this.*

I don't know if he'll remember you, Monroe. He's had his mind fucked with by that bitch Sonya. And he has no memory prior to hooking up with Martin. But he's my friend. And he's saved me on more than one occasion now. So if you hurt him, or if you're lying to me, you won't find a hole deep enough nor will you ever be able to hurt anyone ever again. Do you understand me? Monroe was humbled at her threat, and actually sort of frightened too. *I'll tell him, but I'm not making any promises concerning him contacting you. Like I said, he's had a rough time of it.*

I understand. And when you summon Martin, I should very much enjoy being there with you. I have a few more things I'd like to speak to him about as well. She said she'd think about it, and he felt the connection close.

That surprised him as well. He'd contacted her, not the other way around. Usually the caller was the only one that could disconnect a conversation. Monroe looked at the man on the floor and decided that whatever this female was, he was going to enjoy her taking on Martin. He only hoped that Cyrus was indeed safe.

He had been a vampire for a great many decades when he'd come upon the human. He'd been being hanged for a crime he had more than likely done. But there was a connection there, a great one, and Monroe had interceded on his part. Taken the man to his bosom as well as his bed, and they'd been together since. Monroe couldn't remember a time when he'd not been in love with the other man. And converting him had been the only thing he could have done to save him.

When Martin came around, Monroe was waiting. It hadn't been that long, ten minutes or so, but he'd done a lot of planning. One plan was to get the man healthy enough that he'd be around for a bit longer. At least long enough for the female to call him to her. And he'd taken his own precautions as well. He'd taken the vampire's blood to keep track of him. When Martin shied away from him, Monroe laughed.

"You are in such trouble. You know this, correct?" Martin spit at him. He knew his mind now, and Martin had hoped that Monroe would end his life rather than keep at him the way he had been for the last two days. "You will not anger me now. I have talked with someone that knows you, and they are royally pissed. I think, if I were you, I'd find me a nice sunny place and have myself a sunbath. Until you are no more."

"I'm going to be around for a long time, you son of a bitch." Monroe snapped his fingers, and he watched as the man's leg broke in several places. As he screamed out in pain, Monroe watched him. He also wondered of the woman Sonya and what issue she had with the female. There was much about her in the man's head, and a great deal about a family called Lanning. As well as a queen. None of it meant anything to him, so he had no answers for the woman as to why Martin or Sonya was after her. "As soon as I come into my power, I'm going to fucking kill you with my bare hands."

"You think so? I do not." He snapped his fingers again and listened as the screams died down. "You see, I have made a decision about you. Not one that you're going to like, but one that I think I shall enjoy a great deal. I am going to leave you to yourself. You'll not be able to do a great many of the things you did before. I have taken the liberty, a small one as it turns out, and have removed your cock too. The raping of your children is done. You will no longer use that part of your body against them. And there will be no more feeding upon them either. That is, as you well know, strictly forbidden by our rulers."

"I don't give a fuck about rules that don't apply to me and my needs. You will return me as I was before. You hear me? And stay the fuck out of my business. I will kill and fuck who I want." Monroe said nothing, but Martin seemed to have plenty to say regardless. "I'm am not going to let someone like you destroy what I've worked centuries to achieve. Either end this shit now or you get the fuck away from me."

Monroe was still laughing when he left the man there. His cock had been nothing to remove. It had been so small that he wondered how it had even functioned. No worries now. As he made his way to the outside, he was surprised at it being so close to the sunrise.

His home wasn't close to here, so he made his way to an empty building to rest for the day. He could feel that there weren't many people around, as early as it was, and he doubted the little burg got going much before six. There weren't as many empty buildings as he'd hoped, but he did find one that was being renovated and moved to the sublevels there. He was just settling down, his body closing off to the world around him, when he felt a touch.

He will meet you. But I have to warn you, he doesn't know who you are. Not really. He does have a fondness for books, that much he does know, and that he has received a couple of treasured ones from someone. The female again. He asked her what she meant. *I told him who you were and that you had his books. He said that he has no books that he is aware of. Then as he stood here, he said that he had a bunch of first additions. Most of them had been given to him as gifts. But he doesn't remember from whom.* That explained a great deal. *Are you sure you know who he is?*

He has a wide nasty scar on his neck. When I found him, he was being hanged. I know not what for, only that he was hungry and had more than likely been rightly accused, but I saved him from his death by converting him. It would be about an inch wide, no longer pink because of its age. He felt her fear then. *Is someone there? Are you being hurt? I can come to you if you should need me to.*

No. I'm fine. I...he has a scar, but he said he doesn't remember who did it to him. I have another friend that says she can help him. I don't know if that will help or not, but she said she can have a look into his head to see if he's been fucked with. He said that he'd like that very much. *She won't be here for a few hours. And Cyrus needs to go to bed, as I'm sure you're aware of. I'll let you know what I find out.*

Again, I am in your debt. Should you need me, for any reason, you have only to call my name. I can find you better with blood, but if you are in fear for your life, I will come to your aid. She thanked him, and he lay back down. *I was wondering if you would tell me your name.*

I don't think so. I have enough shit going on without you calling me too. He had to smile. *I'll let you know when I can. Like I said, he's going to bed now.*

I understand. I am there myself. She said nothing, but he could still feel her fear. If he knew her or where she might be, he'd have someone look over her. But for now he'd have to make sure she knew that he was there for her. Closing his eyes, he thought of Cyrus and how he'd found the man.

He'd been hanged, as he'd told her. His horse had been used for the deed. And the men who had strung him up had taken it upon themselves to rid Cyrus of his money, as well as his pocket watch. The watch even now hung in the house where they had lived for so many years. A treasure that reminded them daily of how lucky they were to have found each other. And Monroe had been able to save him.

Monroe had found it; the watch had been in the things that the men who had hurt his love had taken from him that day. They were long dead, of course, their lives shortened considerably when he'd found them in their beds.

Monroe was looking forward to showing it to his friend again once he was home. That was, if he could convince the female that he was indeed his friend and she allowed him to see Cyrus. Monroe rolled to his side, thinking about the woman once again as his body shut down.

CHAPTER 11

Laci held the small notebook in her hand and looked at the safe she'd just opened. There were...well, if she was honest with herself, she wasn't sure what some of the things were. Even with the book to tell her what they were, she had no idea if the unknown item was a saveer or a dangel. Whatever the hell they were. There was an entire list of things she did know too. Others still that she had no idea how to pronounce. Money, however, she understood.

There were, so far as she could see, several stacks of one hundred dollar bills. She'd pulled one of them out and had counted a thousand of them in one bundle. She estimated that there were fifty of those bundles, as well as several bundles of twenties and even fifties. Laci looked up when Nildale came into the room with her.

"I found this." He nodded and sat beside her. He'd come here earlier this morning, telling her that he had needed to get out and about. She wasn't sure now that had been his only reason for being here, but she was really glad that he was here with her now. "You knew that I'd found this, didn't you?"

"Nay, I knew that you found the combination. I had not realized that you knew about the safe until I felt the magic." She asked him about the magic. "'Tis full of it. Well not now, but it was. You have it now. I would imagine that it was meant for you to find, the way it surrounded you and not me too."

"You gave it to me?" He shook his head at her and smiled. She wasn't sure that she really trusted this man yet to ever touch her again, and if he gave her more magic she was going to use it on him to kick his ass. She looked at the safe again and decided to change the subject until she could wrap her mind around what she'd discovered. "I talked to a vampire today. I mean, I think he was one. He said that he knows Cyrus."

"Monroe." She nodded. "He is his maker. I wondered how he'd come to be with Martin, so I looked. Did you know that Sonya has messed with Cyrus's mind as well? I will have Linyah look into getting his memories restored. It will do him a great deal of good to have them back. I cannot do it, as it will bind him to me. I don't want that, and I would think neither does Monroe."

"You didn't say anything before when it came up that Martin claimed to be his maker. Why not?" She stared at the safe again. "There is a lot of money in that sucker too. Did you see it?"

"I did. I believe as the one who has opened it, the money and all contents now belong to you." She shook her head. "I'm sorry child, but that is the way magic works. The finder keeps it. And in this case, you have hit the…motherlode, I think, is the term I need to use. But as for not saying anything about Monroe, I honestly had no idea who Cyrus had been created by. As I said, his mind had been tampered with, and I only thought to see who might have done it."

She nodded. Laci knew that Cyrus was a friend of Nic's, and more than likely he knew who had done the mind scrabble thing to him. Laci also knew that they were working on a timeline. Things happened, she was told, in an order. And to mess with that, even to help a man with his fruit salad mind, was to fuck a lot of things up. She looked at the safe again.

"You can have it. I gift it to you." He smiled sadly at her this time. "I really don't want it, Mr. Nildale. I really have enough of it right now that I can't use."

"Why can't you use it? It's there for you. All of it. I had wondered...you should use it, child. The money and the magic. It's in abundance for you and should you need it, I think you will do well with the knowledge on how to make it work for you." She felt her eyes fill with tears. "I do regret what I did to you that first day. I had only meant to help you...nay, that's not right. I only meant to show off. To a human. It had been so long since I'd seen one, a wholly human being, that I was a smart ass and hurt you."

"I thought you'd killed me." Nildale nodded but said nothing. Reaching for his hand, she took it into hers. She needed contact with him for some reason. "When I was in the kitchen a bit ago, I thought about a chocolate chip cookie. You know the kind. Dunlap, Carter's cook, makes them. I have never had such wonderful.... Anyway, I thought of one. Just one. Or a dozen."

He laughed. "I often find that I cannot eat just one of them either. It is as if he had put some drug in them to make you crave more of them. I think I should like a tin of them now."

It just appeared with them as she thought of the tin she'd found on the table when she'd thought of having one. Nildale looked at the tin for several seconds. Then keeping his hand wrapped around hers, he opened the box and handed her two of them. As if something like this happened every day.

"It does for me. Happens daily. I am not a man who does without." He ate two while he spoke. "Once I tried to get this sandwich to me. I had no idea where it had come from. Kendra had been on this earth for a few days and had brought one of them with her to the castle. She, of course, shared, but I couldn't get the thought of its flavor out of my head. So I did a search for any and all sandwich places around the Lanning compound. It was a large failure on my part."

"I don't suppose you thought to ask her about it." He asked her what sort of fun that would have been. "I see. A man who likes to indulge himself, as well as a man who likes an adventure. So how many did you have before you broke down and asked her?"

"Seventeen. Some of them weren't so bad. Others I couldn't even take the first bite. There was one in particular that had cooked the tomato and lettuce right on the sandwich." He ate four more cookies. Laci wondered if he ever put on weight. "I don't. And neither do you. And you should also know that while I'm not looking in your head, since we are holding hands, I cannot help but see your thoughts on a less than personal level."

She jerked her hand from his, and he laughed as he pulled it back to his. He asked her for more cookies, and she thought of the tin full to overflowing. Nildale said thanks and munched them down as they sat there. A glass of cold milk, too, appeared and she figured that he'd had something to do with that. Laci leaned back against the desk she was sitting in front of and looked down at the little notebook she'd found.

"It says here that there is over ten million in cash at last count. I think there is a little more." He said there was. "Why on earth would someone put that much money in that thing and never use it? And the other things. I don't understand what most of it is, but I'm sure that he could have used it as well."

"I'm sure that he thought he'd live for a very long time. But, alas, things did not go as he had planned." She asked him if he knew the person. "Nay, it's there, in your head. You know of him. When you opened the safe, the contents not only held the things listed there but his story. Close your eyes and you can see it."

She wasn't ready for that and told him so. "I would like to know what you meant by the magic. You said it was there, it's why you came here."

"I knew of the safe and that you'd found it. Max had asked me to watch for it. I think he knows a great deal about it as well, but he told me that he didn't know the contents. It was locked from him. I was only here in the event that it wasn't what we had thought. It turns out that it wasn't, but so much more. You are very gifted, child, because of this. As is Andrew." She asked him what he meant. "The two of you are connected, in all things. You feel pain. He does as well. When there is magic given to one of you, both of you shall receive it. The knowledge on how to use it comes to both of you, and you will share that information as well. I can help you, and in turn, Andrew as well."

"Help me how? And if you mean zap me again, no thanks. I might hurt you this time." He nodded and ate two more cookies before the tin disappeared. "You shouldn't be eating only sweets. You need real food."

"I love sweets. All magical creatures do. Something about the drain on us that can be replaced by eating sugary things." She asked him if he'd been drained. "No, I was just hungry for some cookies this time. But when you crave it, you should eat it. Your body will know when you are depleted."

She stood up and looked deeper into the safe. It was a huge fucker. She thought it to be about six foot tall and about that wide. The doors, double ones that opened with a single combination, stood wide open now, and she turned on the flashlight that suddenly appeared in her hand. Laci didn't even look at Nildale when he laughed.

"You are learning even now. Perhaps I was wrong to think that you needed my help. You might just be better at this than I first thought." Laci told him she wasn't so sure. "You are, my dear. Trust me, you are."

There were vials of things, all of them marked and some in a language that she didn't know. There were bars of what appeared to be soap and the label on two of them, bruyère it said, the French word for heather, was there as well. She wondered aloud what one would use a block of heather for.

"The seeds. Someone went to a great deal of trouble to dry them and then bundled them for the seeds. If you look at the bars, you can see that they're wrapped tightly in some sort of mesh material and not something one would find in soap." She nodded, seeing it now. Nildale got up and stood on the other side of her as they peered into the safe. "I see there are some other herbs too. Most of them gone from this realm but grown in fields on my own lands. I should think that you'd make a fortune on them should you start sprouts and sell them."

"Do you think that is what the man was doing with them?" Nildale said that he doubted it. "Yeah, me either. If he had this much cash laying around to stuff in here, I'm pretty sure he could have afforded a double cheese burger and a large malt."

"Yes, I would imagine that he could have afforded steak should he have wanted it as well. But heather is a big component in a great many spells. The things in the vials too are used in magic." Laci looked at the stacks of other items, some of them wrapped in parchment paper, others in what looked like leather. Reaching for one of those now, she moved the knife on top of the pile.

She saw the man, the one putting the things in the safe, when she touched her finger to the long blade. He was sad, she knew as well. He knew that his betrayal, whatever it might be, was going to get him killed. She also knew in that moment what he was.

"He was a witch. A strong one it seems. And very sad." Nildale asked her if she could see his face. "Yes. He's older, gray hair and beard. But it's well-trimmed, not like you see in the movies. His eyes are a brilliant shade of purple. He looks like he's injured. I think he's stolen the money and things here. Whatever he's doing, it's taken a great deal from him. I can feel his weakness that has little to do with his magical power."

"He would be strong to have put his magic in here for safe keeping. And if he's stolen the money, as you said, it more than likely is why he'd never gotten the chance to use what he has stored here." Laci watched the man as he put more things in it. Then it occurred to her that she wasn't watching him so much as she was doing it with him.

"I'm him. Before when I picked up the bracelet, I never realized that I was the one that was being hit. I just thought...I guess it's silly to have thought that, but I thought that I was watching things from afar." Nildale said nothing more as she saw the witch stacking money in the safe. "He's talking. No, that's not right. He's putting a spell on things. I don't know what he's saying, but it feels like he's putting the magic on each thing he puts in the safe."

When he was finished and closed up the large doors, he walked to the far wall. She could see the rooms now; it had been a storage area of sorts. There were drying herbs hanging from the long wooden boards above her head even now. A bed was only a sheet lying over what appeared to be straw on the floor. There was even a fire ring, its flame small and smokeless as it burned. When he came to a mirror, an oval shaped one that she'd seen in one of the rooms on the upper floors, she looked at the man staring back at them.

"He's older than I thought. I can see him now. He has lines beside his eyes, as well as his skin looks tired. He has been around for a very long time, and the years haven't been good to him." She wasn't surprised when he reached up and touched his finger to his cheek that she could feel it too. "Nildale, I can feel him."

"You have a connection to him now. Not just with the blade but with the things you found in his hiding place." When the man began to speak, it took her several seconds to realize he was speaking in Latin. She translated it for Nildale.

"'I shall be dead soon. Much sooner than I had hoped. But I have left you something. It's there in the safe for you to use should you...you will need it. There is a man that will come to you. He will offer you so much but ask for nothing in return. Take his knowledge. You will need it.'" Laci felt something move over her and stopped talking to Nildale. The man continued as if he were speaking directly to her. "'You are the soul of my magic. And when you are able to understand all, you will also understand the reasons behind the things that have been set in motion for you. Laci Lanning, you are going to save a great many people. And Nildale, the king, he will help you understand.'"

Laci felt the darkness simply swallow her up.

~~~

Andrew wanted to murder Nildale. Not that he'd hurt Laci, but because he'd been with her instead of him when she'd fallen ill. More than that, he wanted the man to suffer as he was. Laci wasn't waking up and no matter what he did, she continued to lay there. Andrew picked her hand up into his and held it to his cheek.

"I don't know what to do. I really want you to wake up, love. What am I going to do without you? You need to wake for me love. You're my heart." He felt his eyes fill with tears, and he didn't even bother with wiping them away or even hiding them from his family. "Laci, please come back to me."

Andrew and Max had settled in a hotel after leaving the last string of houses. They'd gotten some really good deals, but they were both tired. After eating a fast dinner, they'd taken a room and were going to bed soon so that they could get an early start in the morning. As soon as he got out of the shower, he felt her. Then nothing.

"She's hurt. Laci's been hurt." Max stood up as well, his jammies bright in the dimly lit room. "I have to go. We have to go. Something has happened."

"I'm coming. You go now. I'll have someone come back for the car." He nodded, unsure of what to do. "Go, Uncle Andrew, go now."

That had been two days ago, and nothing had changed since he'd found her on the floor in the sublevels of the antique store. Nildale had been holding her hand and screaming for her to come back when he'd picked her up and held her to him. Andrew took her to his house and had put her here. Nildale told him what had happened.

"She was standing in front of the wall to the offices. Before that she'd been telling me what the man was saying. Then she stopped. I have no idea if he did or not, whoever this man was, but then suddenly she was falling to the floor and I couldn't wake her." The man had been devastated, as he was since they'd come here. Sina and Kendra had come to them as well. Even Tristin came and went, but no one could help.

"I've had Linyah look. She's not hurting or unhealthy, but her mind is a jumble of things right now and she said it's hard to capture just one thing that has her out like this." He nodded at Misha. "Did she contact you before?"

"No. I got this trickle of something. Like she was happy, then sad. I started to ask her if she was all right, but then she was happy again. I guess I should have talked to her, but we were at this house and I just wanted to finish up and get back to her." Misha said he more than likely would have done the same thing. "I don't know what to do for her. She's so quiet right now."

"I don't either. And I went by the building to look into that safe, but it's all locked up. Nildale said he didn't close it, so I have no idea what happened there." Andrew didn't know anything about the safe but nodded. "There was a notebook with her. Max wants to know if you have it."

He handed him the little leather book and held Laci's hand again. He hadn't even looked at it, so he had no idea if it was important or not. When he heard Max speak to him, he looked over at him and wondered where his family had gone.

"They are near. I asked them if I could talk to you." Andrew told him now wasn't a good time. "It's about what's wrong with Laci."

"You know?" He said that he didn't for sure, but he wanted to talk to him. "I'm really kind of talked out, Max. If you can't help her, I'd really like to be left alone, please."

"The magic that she got from the safe, it's yours now too." Andrew nodded, not really caring. "You can see what she saw before she passed out. It's right there. It was meant for her, I think. But since you are mated to her, it's yours as well."

"The safe she found in the basement? She told me that she found a book. Is that it, the one Misha gave you?" He said that it was. "And you knew that this was going to happen?"

"No. Had I even known that she was going to open it, I would have told her to wait. She did this...I think she had to do this." Andrew asked him what he meant. "I think whatever was in the safe was meant for her. And when she found the combination, she had to open it. Not wanted, but had to."

"Do you think it was to harm her?" Max said that he didn't think so. "But look at her, Max. Something happened that has put her out like this. I don't know what you know, but it would really help me if you could tell me what is hurting my mate like this."

"Uncle Andrew, I don't think she's hurting. But I think her mind is dealing with something that she saw when she looked at the wall. And all the magic that she got. Nildale said that he'd felt it, the magic, but he never got any of it. Whatever had been inside the safe, she got it all to share with you." Andrew looked at Laci as Max continued. "Something was there that was too much for her. Or she saw something that the man saw or did."

"She told me about the bracelet. And how she was connected somehow to it. You think she touched something in the safe that she connected to?" He said that he didn't know but he thought perhaps she had. "And you think I can look too? You mean go into her mind and see what she did? And you think this will help her to wake up?"

"It's worth a shot. Linyah said her mind was jumbled. Maybe you can calm it by just being there for her." Andrew asked him how to do it. "Just connect with her as you do when you speak to her. I think that on the level that the two of you speak, she's there waiting for you. Like I said, I don't know for sure, but it can't hurt either of you to try."

He'd tried when he'd first brought her here but had hit a wall. Andrew was willing to do anything to have her back with him. Kissing her hand and curling his fingers into hers, he took a long breath in and let it out slowly.

At first all he could feel was emotions. Sadness. Happiness. Love. Depression, and even felt her being overwhelmed by a great many things. But the deeper he moved through them, the less and less he could feel of her emotions but found memories. Her parents. Her aunt and the upcoming trial. There was a puppy that she adored that had been killed, as well as the day her parents had been taken from her. The memories weren't in any sort of order, but he thought that they made sense to her. A timeline of her own making. Then he saw the man.

"He's there. I think it's him. He looks older than us, even older than Nildale. He's putting things in the safe." Max told him that was more than likely it, that Nildale told him what Laci had seen with him. "Money and vials. I don't know what they are, but I can see them all. Jewels as well. In large leather pouches that are on the bottom in the back, there are things she didn't look at. It looks as if she touched very little of what is in it. And there is a blade."

"She mentioned that too." He didn't move from his positon when he heard Nildale speak softly. "That's when she moved over to the wall. She said he was speaking Latin. And she told me what he was saying to her."

As they made their way to the wall, he could see the mirror there and commented that he'd seen it before. But when the man was standing there, he sort of faded out and became Laci. Andrew watched her carefully in the reflection.

He said that he put the safe here for me. Andrew asked her why. *I don't know. He told me that I was the soul of his magic. And when I was able to understand everything, then I would also understand the reasons behind the things that have been set in motion for me. Then he called me Laci Lanning, like he knew that I was going to meet you. And that Nildale could help us understand all the magic that we got. That we were to let him help us.*

Anything else? She told him about saving people. *Who? Did he say that? Did he also explain to you how to get you to come back to me? I'm so worried about you.*

We have more magic now. I know that much, and with it we can do a lot more shit than we could before. Andrew, I'm not sure I can handle more magic. He told her they'd be all right. *If you say so. I'm not sure how to come back to you though. It's as if I'm in this flux state. I can hear you all, but I can't seem to move.*

I'll work on that. She told him to hurry. *I will love. I promise you I will. Just don't go anywhere. I need you too.*

When he moved out of her mind, seeing things that he was pretty sure he'd not noticed before, he also felt her magic. It was hers...he had no doubt about that. And when he leaned back in his chair again, he looked at Max.

"She's all right, like you said, but she can't seem to wake up. She also said she can hear us. But there's...she has this power now that I never felt before. And for whatever reason, I don't think I'm supposed to get a part of it. It's for her." Neither Max nor Nildale said anything as he sat there. "She also said that the man told her that we were to let Nildale help us with the magic. I'm not sure what that means, but she might when she wakes up."

"I will do whatever I can to help you both. You know that." Andrew nodded at Nildale. "The mirror, do you suppose we should return it to the wall where she spoke to the man? It might be the connection that she needs later."

"I don't know. She was there, in the mirror for me to talk to." Nildale only glanced at Max but said nothing. "If that means something to you, right now I don't care. I'm too exhausted to wonder what that might be about."

Andrew felt calmer having talked to her. He closed his eyes, thinking only to rest them, when he felt his body simply give under the weight of the last week. Andrew felt like a man drowning as the heavy need to sleep took him.

CHAPTER 12

Martin moved from one end of his office to the other. He hurt. Even to breathe pained him so badly that he knew that he had broken ribs that were sticking in part of him that they shouldn't. His legs too, both of them, were not right. The way they had set up on their own made him think that he'd never walk well again. Whatever the monster was that hurt him, he was going to pay for it.

Several times since he'd woke to find himself in the middle of his lair floor, he'd tried to think who or even what it was that had hurt him. Sometimes, at the oddest times, he'd think it was a man. Then others still he thought of a woman. The woman, however, scared him much more than the man did, even for all his apparent strength and power that seemed to come with the memory of him.

Cyrus was there too, though at what capacity he had no idea. But fear him he did. Again, not as much as the woman, but he did shiver when he thought of Cyrus. He'd even tried to find him again. Cyrus had been lost to him somehow, but Martin didn't think that he was dead. And if he was honest with himself, he really wasn't sure that he wanted to find him again. Fear had him shying away from that.

He heard a noise behind him, like a door slamming in the house, and he flinched away from the sound. Screaming from the pain in his legs again, he felt sweat bead on his forehead and reached up to touch it. Never, not even before he'd hit his maturity, had Martin ever remembered sweating for any reason.

Martin had grown up privileged. Not to say that his parents were as rich as he was now, but they'd had money to use and spend on the family. Even as a child, Martin had made sure that whatever was spent on him and his brothers, he got more than his fair share. Even if he had to take it from his brothers by beating them to shit.

He also knew that as the third born son to his father that he was really entitled to nothing. But he wanted it no less. Simply because he was Martin Richards, last in line to get the estate if anything should happen to his two brothers, didn't mean that he should have to find his own way in the world, not when it was all right there for the taking. And Martin, as he did now, thought he should get it all.

His father had already appointed his brother, who was older than him by nearly eighty years, to be the overseer to most things on the estate. Even his second brother, also older by nearly forty years, had a great deal of responsibility with the way things were going to be run, as well as how the money was going to be settled when his parents had had enough of life.

Martin had done what he'd wanted, who he wanted before that, and saw no reason for him to change things because his father was bowing out. Almost as soon as his brothers were in charge of things, his life started to not progress the way he'd wanted. He was no longer pampered, but if he wanted something he now had to work for it. Meaning he was no longer given the best of everything. His brothers said they were saving for a rainy day, that maybe they'd not always have the kind of money they had now. Well, fuck that shit. He didn't care if a monsoon had come on. He hated their new rules.

Martin didn't want to have to work for anything. To him it should have been his because he said so. Even now he hated the word no. And when he heard it, Martin would lose his temper. Few survived when he let his anger get the better of him.

"I should have had what I wanted, without all those rules." So at the tender age of fourteen, a full decade before he was to be a full vampire, Martin hired a bunch of thugs to enter his home and kill his family. They were really of no use to him by then anyway. Even now he was saddened. Not by their deaths, no, but that the money hadn't been as plentiful as he'd been led to believe.

As he turned to start back down the long room, he saw his reflection in the tall mirror. Something had happened to his face when he'd been out. It had taken him nearly an entire day to convince himself that it wasn't a trick in his reflection, but that someone had branded his face with a blade or claw of some sort. Each time he'd looked at himself, he would be horrified that he'd been hurt like this. Martin was going to make someone pay for this. And his cock.

Martin had been putting on clean clothing when he felt a pain in his balls. At first he'd thought it the need to urinate, a feeling that he'd not had in a very long time. Anything that he took into his body was used up. There had been nothing for him to void out of his body for centuries. As he'd made his way to his bathroom, stripping off his clothing as he went, Martin heard a man's laughter and he felt his balls tighten closer to his body.

Going into the bathroom and closing and locking the door behind him, he hid in the shower stall for twenty minutes before he let his legs stretch out in front of him. That was when he noticed that his cock was gone.

There was no wound there. Not even a scar to indicate that there had ever been an appendage he'd ruled women and men with. He touched the area where his balls were and felt them full, but his cock was simply gone. A flittering thought ran through his head again. A man's laughter again and someone telling him that he had a small dick, but it didn't stay there long enough for him to capture the exact time he'd been mutilated.

Martin had gotten up then. Stood on the counter in his bath to search his entire body for his cock. He'd even looked at the bottom of his feet, in his ass, and on his back. Nothing. He made his way back to where he'd been when he woke and looked around the area as well.

No blood on the floor. There was no knife or any kind of weapon that would have cut him through like that. After a thorough search of his body, he tore apart his room. The bed, the mattress. He even tore the curtains from their rods. Lifted rugs that had been scattered around the room. Martin had even gone as far as to look in the fireplace grate to see if it had been put there.

The search of his home took longer. Every person he met, he asked if they'd seen his cock. Two of the girls in the kitchen had giggled and he lashed out at them, tearing both their heads from their bodies and leaving them where they died.

It was gone. No trace of it anywhere in his home or his person. And he had no idea how or when it had happened. Now he was reduced to pacing his own hallway trying to work the soreness out of his body. There didn't seem to be any relief to that either. No matter that he'd nearly drained four of his staff for fresh blood. Nothing helped.

Cyrus. The name entered his head like a small fly buzzing around his head. Stopping where he was, he was just reaching the end of his walk when the man's face appeared. Taken aback by the sheer size of the man, he fell back on his ass and hit his head as he took a long tumble down the staircase. Blackness took him.

When he woke, finding himself sprawled out on the stairs still, he lay there for several minutes to try and get his bearings. He was in a great deal of pain, yes. But that could have been from his fall. Reaching carefully to his cock, he sobbed hard enough to give himself more pain when he found nothing there. It hadn't been a dream after all.

"I'm not small." He had no idea where the thought came to him that someone thought his cock tiny and that was the reason they'd cut it off. He was huge. Women adored his cock. And when he fucked them with it, they screamed out their delight. But no one had ever said he was small. Not and lived to say it a second time.

Rolling to his side to get up he nearly just lay there, thinking he'd be better off if the sun took him. But the name Cyrus came to him again, fluttering through his head again like he should remember it. If not the man behind the name, then the name itself.

The man standing in front of him had him crying out again, but he didn't black out this time. Martin asked him who he was and what the fuck he wanted. The man only looked at him from head to toe, and Martin thought he found him lacking.

"You have unfinished business." He wanted to ask him what it was. For the life of him he couldn't remember anything he should be doing, but the man spoke again.

"When she calls to you, and she will, do not doubt that, you will go."

"Who? I don't go anywhere I don't want to." The man laughed. "Who the fuck are you? And what the hell are you doing in my house?"

"Nic." He said that as if that explained it all. "I've come to make sure that you are fit enough to go to her. She will need to end your life, and it would be better if she didn't have to feel guilty that killing you would be a blessing to you."

"What the fuck are you saying? Are you saying that you want me better so that when I go to this woman so she can kill me, it'll be less painful for her?" Martin didn't even wait for an answer, stupid as it would have been. "What are you on? Because if you think this is something that I'm willing to do, then you're nuttier than a fucking cake."

"You'll have no choice in the matter. When she calls, and she will as I have said, then you will go to her. She has the power to call any vampire to her. Something that we did not know when we gave her magic." Martin nodded, then shook his head. "You're confused."

"No shit. I have my own brand of magic by the way. I'm just too weak to show you just how much I have." He felt his legs move, the bones that had been out of place straightened and got stronger. The pain made his belly sick, his head spin. "What are you doing to me? Make it stop now. It fucking hurts."

"Of course it does. You don't expect yourself to be repaired without some sort of pain, do you?" Martin wanted to get up and knock the hell out of the man. At the very least, he wanted to tear his throat out. "You cannot harm me. Even if you could, I'd only have to kill you and that won't help us. You must die as it is written."

"Help you what? Die? The only thing I can see going on here is that you're making a lot of assumptions." He laughed, feeling stronger all the time. "You really don't think I'm going to go with this bitch and let her kill me, do you? And what sort of help do you think my supposed death is going to do for you? I'm a great man."

"You are nothing. But your death will be a beacon for others. It will send a message out to others that the Lannings are not a group of beings to mess with." He had heard the name before. Lanning meant something. He just wasn't sure he knew what. "They are a group of leopards that are going to change the world for all paranormals one day soon. And by killing you, it will show others, men like you that fuck with them, as you have called it, that they will die. And not well either."

Martin was lifted up. The man never touched him, but he knew that it was him taking him from the stairs. When he stood on his own feet, he could feel his body working to be stronger, his mind no longer lingering in pain but thinking and planning. Reaching for the man, just to show him who was boss, Martin watched as his hand moved through his body, as if he wasn't really there.

"I am not. And now that you've figured it out, you should also know something else. I did not say that you would go with her, I said that she would summon you. As if she were a necromancer. And once you are there, you will pay the price of each of the deaths that you have caused." Martin laughed. He had been around a very long time and knew for a fact that no one, unless you created them, could call a vampire to them. "You think so? Then I will wish you luck with your meeting."

An hour later, less really, Martin felt like the king of the world. His body felt wonderful, his blood racing in his veins.

Reaching down for his cock, thinking to find him a harem of women, he came up empty handed. His cock was still gone.

"I cannot repair what was taken from you. And even if I could, I think it fitting for a dickless man like you to have to die like you are. Painfully and not whole." The man's voice, Nic's voice, seemed to echo around the room. "You would do well to save your strength, Martin. She will be calling for you soon."

"Fuck her and the horse she rode in on." Martin made his way to his rooms, taking the stairs back up them two and three at a time. He was going out. He might even change him a couple of dozen people tonight and have them come here and serve him. Martin was back, he thought, and dressed in his best suit to go out and conquer some of this world.

~~~

Laci knew the moment that she woke that she wasn't alone in the bed. The warmth behind her seemed to curl around her in much the same way as the blanket that lay over them both. Reaching behind her, she felt his fingers curl into hers and she smiled in the darkened room.

"I didn't think you'd ever wake up." She rolled to her back to look up at Andrew. "Christ, you scared the shit out of me. Don't ever do that again."

"I won't." Laci brushed the hair from his eyes and smiled again. "You held me. Not just with your arms but your love as well. I think that's what brought me back."

"I had to hold you or go insane. Or I guess insaner. How do you feel now?" Laci told him great. "I'm so glad. Christ, I was terrified."

His body rocked into hers and she felt herself respond to him. When he leaned down and kissed her, it was all she could do not to roll him to his back and take him. Running her hand down his chest, she found his bare chest hot, his nipples hard. And when he moaned as she pinched them, she felt her pussy soak.

"What do you want?" She told him that she wanted him. "I can feel that. But what do you want me to do to you? Or with you? I want you to be pleased."

"Fuck me." He shook his head and told her to tell him what she wanted. "I want to ride you, feel your cock deep in my pussy while I ride your cock."

He rolled to his back and she sat up. His cock was thick, precum was dripping from his tip, and she wanted to taste him. Leaning over him, she licked him and nearly cried out when he wrapped his hand into her hair and pushed her head over him again.

"I need to feel your mouth over me first." She didn't mind and took him. "Christ, that's it. Yes, baby, that's perfect."

His cock was so large that it barely fit in her mouth. When he started to fuck her this way, his cock moving in and out of her mouth, she moved to be between his legs so she could touch him as she wanted. The harder he rode her mouth, the more she explored. Her hands were touching him anywhere she could, and he seemed to like it.

His balls were full and heavy when she cupped them in her hand. Hot too. Laci wanted to taste them as well and took one of them in her mouth. He nearly took her head off when he jerked her head up from him, and she thought she'd hurt him.

"You do that again and I'm going to come all over you. And that is not the way I want to feel my cock explode right now." She pouted at him. "Do you have any idea how...? No, you don't. It's like you stuck my balls in a light socket and it felt fucking amazing. I swear, if I wasn't so close now, I'd let you have your fun, but I want to feel your pussy wrapped around my cock."

"I'm going to suck your balls sometime. I think I'd like for you to come all over me too. Feel your cream on me." He moaned twice as she made her way up his body. "I want to feel your cum on my body. I want to watch it as it spills from you onto me."

"I can do that." He fisted his cock while she settled over him. "Slowly, baby. If you go quickly, I'm not going to last."

Laci dropped over him, and his cock filled her from the back of her throat to her feet. He cried out, holding her hips when she started to ride him, and she knew that he was losing his control. Leaning over him, she took his nipple in her mouth and bit down hard.

He cried out again that he was coming. Andrew threw her on the bed and onto her back. As soon as she was there, he fucked her, hard pounding strokes that gave her little relief to her own need. When he bowed back, his body nearly horizontal to her own, he snarled, his cat moving all over his body as he did. And when he moved off her with the same quickness that he'd taken her, she saw his cat take his body like he'd swallowed him whole.

The cat wasted no time in burying his mouth over her. He ate her like she was his last meal, and he was going to make a feast of it. His tongue fucked her, curling deep inside of her, making her think he was mining for some part of her he'd not tasted as yet.

He bit her, his teeth making marks on her thighs and legs. His paws dug deep into her skin, leaving his prints all over her. Still he ate her, fucked her with his tongue, bringing her so many times that she was weak with it, her body so drained she thought that he'd sucked her dry.

Then he stood up, his paws on either side of her. His face was only inches from hers as he stood over her. She saw him there. Andrew was with him, just below the surface of his eyes. He was looking at her too, through the eyes of his great cat. And when he moved back, the big cat taking his body from hers, she watched him move to the floor and stand near the bed.

"What is it?" Andrew said he had no idea. When she tried to stand, his cat knocked her back, his paw careful of her skin now but keeping her there. "I don't understand what you're doing. I want you to come back to me."

He won't let me. I can't get him to release me. She asked him why not. *I don't know, love. But he wants you to stay where you are.*

"I'm afraid, Andrew. Make him stop." Almost as if he understood her, and there wasn't any reason to believe that he might not, the cat turned to her and laid his head on her thigh. Laci rubbed her hand through his fur. "He's so beautiful. I love your cat."

The purring made her rub him down his sides. And when he moved his head from her lap and leapt up on the bed, she laid down beside him and held him to her. It wasn't sexual, even though she was naked, but comforting. She asked Andrew if he knew what had happened.

Believe it or not, he just wants you to hold him. I think he missed you as well. Laci held him tighter, keeping his warm body close to her. *He needed this. I think he needed this as much as I do when I hold you in my arms.*

He held her for another hour. Laci and Andrew talked about the things that she'd seen in the safe and the magic that was supposed to be hers. The cat never moved away from her, nor did he hurt her, but only licked her face occasionally as if he were kissing her.

Max and his grandmother are looking for the man's face. My mom is helping too, but she's more of the old school kind of looking. She has some books that they had printed up for her. Laci asked who they thought he was. *They don't know for sure, but Max thinks if he had magic, even back then, someone would have written his name down in the records that the Doran keep.*

"But that doesn't explain how he knew my name. Not just my name, but that I'd be with you, a Lanning." The cat seemed to feel her stress and purred a little louder for her. "I have no idea why, but that sound makes me want to take a long nap. Do you suppose that's why he does it?"

It would be my guess. Andrew laughed. *I just thought of something. When Murph was working, Nic came to her and saved her life. Then he looked up at the cameras that were throughout the house and told Carter – he called him by name – but he told Carter that he'd saved her for him. I wonder if this is the same kind of thing. Someone helping us out by keeping you safe.*

"But I wasn't in trouble there. I mean, I don't think so. Nildale was there, and he would never harm me." She knew that now. And she felt badly for not trusting the man more. "Do you suppose that has anything to do with this Sonya person? That they knew she was sending people out to get me?"

I think so.

The big cat stood up on the bed then stretched out. His claws bit deeply into the mattress but never tore it. When he seemed satisfied with whatever, he nodded. Andrew was suddenly there, and the cat was gone. He pulled her into his arms and held her to his body.

"Now I need to hold you." She was all right with that as well.

CHAPTER 13

"So you think this man, this Monroe, is really Cyrus's maker, and that I can call him to me too." Misha nodded. Andrew wasn't sure this was such a great idea, but before he could voice his concerns again, Laci spoke. "Why the hell would I do that? What if he's no better than the man who claimed him in the first place?"

"I don't think he is, my lady." Andrew looked over at Cyrus. The man had been at her side every night since she woke, standing guard right outside their door as if he expected an attack at any minute. "More and more memories are coming to me. Not all of them about Monroe, but about the books. I received one from him at my birthday one year. I remember being so excited. I don't remember the title, but I remember vaguely that there was someone I greatly respected and loved."

"I don't want you hurt again." Cyrus nodded but said nothing to Laci. When she looked at Andrew, he knew she was going to ask what he thought she should do.

"Call him. There are enough people around here that can take his ass out if he doesn't act like a man reunited with his child." Laci looked at Misha, then back at Cyrus. "He just wants this to be done, love. Not that he wants anyone hurt."

"All right, but if this shit gets real, I'm going to be the first to tell you I told you so." Misha laughed and told her he'd not say a word if she did. "Yeah, like that's going to happen. You have to have the last word about everything."

Misha tried hard not to have a comment. Andrew could see it on his face. Even their mom seemed to find it funny that he was trying to keep his mouth shut. But in the end, Misha had to be Misha.

"I do not have to have the last word. Especially if you just do as I tell you in the first place." He looked at Andrew. "If you laugh, I will tear you up. I'm not like that."

"Sure you're not." Laci looked at him and winked. "Okay, I'm calling him now, but I swear to you, one false move and I'm going to use some of this new crap that seems to be oozing out of my fucking skin."

"I swear to you I want to get a bar of soap after you every time I have a conversation with you." His mom looked at him. "I know that you're no better when you think I'm not listening to you. I want someone not to have such a potty mouth. Or I'll start cursing myself. How do you think that would go over if I used the word fuck like it were a comma?"

She might have gotten away with being stern if she hadn't said fuck in a near whisper. Andrew felt his eyes water and his ribs hurt with trying not to laugh, and completely lost it when Rider laughed.

They were all laughing when a large man appeared in the room. Naked. No one said a word, not even him. He just took the towel that was over his shoulder and wrapped it around his waist before he looked around the room. Laci stood up when he looked at Cyrus.

"Touch him and I will kill you." The man, Monroe he assumed, only nodded. He did put out his hand to Laci, and she stepped back from it. "Sorry, but the last couple of times that I took someone's hand, I was zapped to shit and then knocked on my ass. If it's all the same to you, we'll just skip that part. We'll just pretend that we've gone through the ritual of exchanging handshakes if it's all the same to you."

"You must be Monroe. The vampire that claims to be Cyrus's maker." He turned to Misha and nodded once. "He doesn't remember you yet. And to be honest with you, even though we could help him along with that, we were afraid to do so in the event that whatever was hidden from him was going to be a bad thing."

"We were together for a great many years. The two us came together out of necessity, but grew to love each other very much." Monroe turned to look at Cyrus. "I have never stopped searching for you. I have kept your things the way you left them. Your books on the shelf where you put them in order of the date you received them. The copies of the newer books mixed with the old. I cannot believe that after all these years, you are finally here. So close that I could touch you."

"I'm very sorry, but could you please get dressed?" Andrew looked at his mom when she interrupted Monroe. "You seem like a very nice man, and I'm sure that Laci had no idea that you might have been in such a state of undress when she called to you. At least that's what I'm going to assume. But I'm an old woman who really isn't a prude, but someone who enjoys a man to be wearing more than a towel when having a conversation. Please."

The suit seemed to be as much a part of the man as the towel had been. And when his mom nodded and thanked

Monroe, he bowed before her and smiled. He turned to Laci then, his face unreadable.

"I had a thought that you'd be beautiful. I can see now that I was clearly wrong. You are simply the most beautiful creature that I have seen in a great many year." Andrew stepped beside her. "I meant no harm, sir. I only wished to tell her that she is beautiful. And to thank her for what she's done for me."

"He was being beaten when I thought of him. I didn't want to see him in any more pain after what he'd done to help us at the pharmacy." Andrew was sure that Monroe had no idea what Laci was talking about but he thanked her again. When Linyah appeared in the room, Andrew touched his hand to Monroe's arm when he reached for what he assumed was a weapon.

"You don't want to piss her off by shooting at her." He looked at him. "Linyah will have your head off your shoulders before your heart will beat a second time. Trust me when I tell you, you're better off just letting her do her thing. And she means him no harm. Hopefully it is within her power to help him."

Linyah nodded her thanks to him and touched her fingers to Cyrus's head. In seconds his body went limp and she held him up in one arm as she continued to touch his head. Linyah looked at Monroe as she continued helping the vampire.

"I put him to sleep, for the pain will be great. Sonya has put a block around certain memories that he had, and he could not have breached them on his own. Should he have tried, the memories coming at him even a little would have caused him a great deal more pain than he has now. It is more than likely why he shied away from you reaching out to him." When she pulled her fingers away, she held him out to Monroe. "He will need a great deal of rest before I will allow him to wake. The memories were made over a long period of time, but they will flood his mind all at once should he wake too quickly. Let him sleep it off."

Monroe held his friend to his chest and kissed him on the forehead. He thanked Linyah, then looked at Andrew and Laci. He looked like a man who had been given a great gift.

"Martin hurt him." Laci said that she didn't know the man but that was what she thought too. "You will bring him here? To your home and kill him? I would if I were you. He is not a man that I would leave to chance."

"Nic said that he is pissed off at someone. I guess that would be you." Monroe smiled and that was answer enough. "He hurt my friend, took him from his family, and then tried to have me killed. Several times. Yeah, his ass is mine."

"I should have liked to have been here when you did it. Killed him with magic that he claims to have." Laci told him she could wait. "Nay, I have many years to catch up on with Cyrus, and find that I no longer have the need to see Martin die. But I would like to make a suggestion with your plans to take him out. Do not bring him into your home as you have me. But in the light of day where he will be...he will be less able to harm you and yours, but no less dangerous."

"You mean let the sun cook him." Monroe laughed and said that was it exactly. "Seems kind of fitting, I guess. I would imagine that he'll suffer a great deal that way."

"The bowels of hell could not be as painful as being in the sun for a vampire. You bring him to the grounds here that are magical, the land here. When he is in the sun, listen to his begging and know that for each of his words, there were tens of thousands more said to him from his victims. I have been in his mind, my lady. There is not an ounce of goodness in him. Kill him. And quickly please. But not too quickly. He should suffer some, I think."

Laci moved forward and touched her fingers to the fallen vampire. Andrew knew that she'd miss him…he'd become a part of their family since being here. And as Laci had said, he'd saved her twice now.

"Take care of him. He's the nicest vampire I've ever met. Not that I've ever met any before you two, but he is by far the nicest." Monroe bowed, then smiled at her. "If you don't mind, I think I would like to shake your hand."

"It will give me a part of you. You have some of me. I still don't know how that works, but you do." She nodded and put out her hand. Monroe looked at him for a brief second, then shifted Cyrus in his arms and put out his own. "You are forever in my heart for helping me this day. And you need only to call out for me and we will come to your aid. I cannot thank you enough."

"You have." Their hands touched and Andrew felt the connection. It wasn't light either. He knew as much about the big vampire as he did his own brothers. More maybe. When he disappeared, Laci fell back into his arms, and he sat down on the couch with her. When she stood up, he knew it was time to take care of Martin once and for all.

~~~

Rider stood beside the rest of them. They'd been ordered to stay on the porch, nicely, but ordered all the same, and not to move unless they saw blood. Their blood, not the vampire's. He wasn't sure how much blood there was going to be from the vamp, but he was standing down for now. Rider looked at Misha when he came out on the porch with his son in his arms.

"Do you think having him out here is a good idea? What if something happens and you have to help them?" Rider knew they thought of him as a worrier. He was fine with that; he knew he was. Someone had to keep them from harming themselves, and if he had to be made fun of to make them safe, so be it. "Where is Hannah? Surely she doesn't approve of this?"

"I do. I think it's a lovely day, and Kelly hasn't been able to be out as much as I'd like." Rider wanted to toss up his hands, but the other day when he'd done that to one of his brothers, he'd been made fun of for hours. Instead, he turned his back on them all. He wasn't going to waste his breath this time.

He looked out over the yard to where Andrew and Laci were standing. Rider thought that someone else should be with them. Nic, he thought. He'd be the perfect person to have there in the event that everything went to shit. And Rider knew that it would. Everything lately, it seemed, came out on the bad end of the spectrum.

There was a tent set up. Not the kind that you'd sleep in, but one of those jobbies that you put over a table when at a picnic. Such a contrast, he thought, a lovely day for a picnic and the killing of a monster. Rider smiled when Andrew kissed his mate, and knew it was time to begin.

"Martin Richards, come to me."

Rider nearly asked her if that was going to work when the man appeared in front of her. He looked like a man who had been used to getting what he wanted and on time too. He smirked at the two of them, crossing his arms over his chest as if he did this sort of thing all the time. Coming out into the sun to speak to some leopards.

Rider had no idea why that thought came to him, but it did. He wondered too if the man had any idea that he was about to die. And soon. But Laci wanted answers first, and she thought that if he had some sort of security blanket, like the tent, then he'd be more apt to think he was getting out of this.

"Who the fuck are you? And how the hell did you call me here? Or is this like with that guy, a trick of some sort?" Laci just laughed, her voice traveling across the yard toward them. "You think this is funny, bitch? It's daylight. You know better than to pull a vampire from his lair."

"Monroe wants to know if you've found your dick yet?" Martin cupped his balls and took a step back from her. Rider felt his own balls tighten up when he thought of what the other man had done to Martin. "He told me it was in plain sight for you. It's kind of small, I guess, so you might have missed it. He said it was wee little, like this."

She put her finger up and pinched about an inch or less between them. Of course, it had the desired effect. Martin lunged at her again. This time he caught some rays of the sun. He nearly fell on his ass getting out of the way. His screams of pain hurt his ears, and Rider wondered what it would be like when he was fully exposed.

"You had better have a damned good reason for—"

"Could you tone it down a little?" The man just looked at her. "My nephews are on the deck up there, and while the rest of us curse like a drunk on leave, you aren't family. And besides, my mother-in-law, Maribel Lanning? She's a sweetheart, by the way, but she doesn't like it either. Just tone it down a little."

"Fuck you. And fuck the rest of you fucking stupid fucking idiots." He flipped them off, and Rider had to laugh. This was by far much more entertaining than he'd thought it would be. "You fucking cunt, tell me what the fuck you want."

Taking a step toward Martin, Laci slammed her fist into his face. Had Rider not been standing there when she did it, he was sure he'd never have believed it. When the vampire fell back this time, he jumped up so quickly that he fell forward again. That was all the time that Andrew needed to have his leopard come out.

Martin didn't move when Andrew moved toward him, his back to the pole at the back of the tent. Rider could almost taste Martin's fear, and was glad now that he'd been told to stay up here. He was sure, like the rest of them, they would have torn the man apart for talking to one of their women the way he had.

"Now. Here is what's going to happen. I'm going to ask you some questions and Andrew here isn't going to eat you. He might yet, but for now, we're going to get some answers. Does that sound like a plan to you?" When he didn't answer her, she commanded him to. The power of it took his breath away. "Answer me."

"Yes. A plan. Is he going to chase me into the sun?" Laci shrugged. "I'll answer your questions, but don't let him chase me. I refuse to die that way."

"Well, that really is too bad now, isn't it? My first question. What did Sonya tell you was the reason for her wanting me killed?" He asked her how she'd found out about that. "I'm very smart. Especially when someone tries to murder me. What was her reason?"

"She said that she didn't want you to become mated to a Lanning." The man seemed to just realize what she'd said earlier about her mother-in-law being a Lanning. "I guess that went to shit. But there is one more of you, so maybe I can fix that one."

Rider felt all their eyes turn to him. His mate. The man was talking about his mate. He wanted to know what their plans for her were, but Laci spoke before he could ask.

"This other woman, what is she? Human? Something more?" He said that he didn't know. "But you and Sonya had a plan to kill her as well? Because of this plan that she had to keep the man unmated."

"We do plan to kill all of you eventually. But Sonya said that so long as even one of you guys didn't have your mate, she'd won. I don't know what it was, but the bitch pays well and that's all I really cared about. Can you have him back the fuck up?" Martin whimpered so loudly that they all heard him when Andrew moved closer to him. "This is not helping me think. Tell him to back off."

"You don't need to think, moron. Just keep telling us what you know. Or I can go in your head and get it. I understand that raping a person's head is pretty painful. I'm not any good at it, but I'm sure you won't mind being my first, would you?" He told her to ask the fucking questions so he could go. "How very kind of you. How much magic did she give you? I'm guessing more than you needed to come and get me. And she funded you as well, didn't she? What happens now?"

"You know about the magic too? Well, fuck. Yeah, she said it was my reward. That and fucking her. She wasn't all that good, but she seemed to think she was." He cupped his balls and made a fucking motion with his other hand. Rider glanced at his mom, but she was watching little Kelly instead of the goings on in front of them. He was sure she could hear him, but for now she wasn't looking.

"I'm sure that the two of you made a lovely couple. Her a caustic bitch and you a dickless wonder. Did you know that she's dead?" Martin nodded. "I see. And so why would you continue on trying to kill the mates to the Lanning men if you knew that?"

"There is more to come to whoever kills the last one of you cunts. It's some sort of spell that she put out there for us to get when the last one is murdered. I was the closest running for it, by the way. There are more of us out there. I just happen to be the one closest to getting to you fuckers." Martin grinned at her when she asked him what sort of spell. "It's in this big fucking safe. I saw it once. Double door sucker that looks like you could hold a few bodies in it. I think I might just stuff yours in it with that other broad when I find her. It'd be fitting I think. But she had this guy load it for her. I don't think he knew what it was for. But he was some old fucker that got a shit load of money and magic. She told me once that when this was done, she was going to enjoy killing him off and taking what should have been hers in the first place. Not sure what that meant, but I'm going to get that magic."

Rider felt the tension around him heat up. There was magic out there, and a great deal of it for someone to kill his mate. He had to grip the railing tightly or go and kill the man. Instead of being upset, Laci laughed. He wondered what she might find so.... Christ. It occurred to him then that Laci had the magic that was supposed to go to the winner of killing his mate. Rider felt both relieved and terrified at the same time.

"You have any information on the other people coming to get us?" Martin said that there were hundreds after them. "No, there's not. There were only four others besides you. Three of which are already dead. Just as you will be soon. Before I do this, I want to tell you thanks. Thanks to you, a great many things are now clearer to me. And we know what we have to work with. Enjoy your time in hell, you fucking asshole. And this is for Cyrus."

189

Martin screamed when the tent rolled back. No one moved as the man seemed to not just catch fire but become the very flame of hell, just as Monroe had said. When his screams were cut off, Rider turned his back with the rest of his family and let the man die alone. He didn't want to see the last seconds of his dying, no matter how afraid he was for his own mate.

When Laci put her hand on his arm, Rider felt the need to hug her. Pulling her into his arms, he held her tightly. Christ, he loved these women, all of them, and was thankful every day that they'd come to them.

"I'm sorry I couldn't get any more information for you." He nodded, his heart too heavy to speak. "Rider, we'll find her. Safely too. She's going to come here, kick your ass, and make you very happy."

"I'd just be happy if she were all right." She nodded and he let her go. "Thank you for what you did. That couldn't have been easy for you."

She nodded and moved away from him. Rider needed a run, he decided. He was making his way to the trees behind the house when he felt someone moving toward him. Rider paused when he saw James coming out of the woods as his big wolf.

I'd like some company if you don't mind joining me. Rider nodded. *I'm having a day — a week really — and could use a good run with a cat. We could beat the shit out of each other too if you don't mind.*

Yeah, sounds like a plan. Stripping off his shirt, he let his cat take him. He was tackling the big wolf even as his pants untangled from his foot. Rider needed something hard, mean, and bloody. James didn't pull back, and the two of them fought like they were ready for murder.

After an hour of both of them giving as good as they got, they ended up by the pond at the end of the property. Rider licked a couple of his wounds clean, glad for the first time that he could heal quickly and not be killed easily. The big wolf hadn't been kidding when he said that he wanted someone to tussle with. When James laughed, Rider asked him if he was all right now.

Better. My wife is pissed at me. Rider didn't ask. If James wanted him to know, then he'd tell him. *She's working for Charlie. Well, sort of working for her. She's been making blankets for her shop. I know that she's having fun at it, and all I said was she should spend the money she makes on herself, not the kids.*

I don't understand. Why would that make her pissed off at you? I mean, she made the money, right? Why shouldn't she get herself something for all her hard work? James said that's what he thought. *But she didn't think so.*

No. James sat there for several more minutes, and Rider was thinking of mates and the strangeness of them. *I don't air my problems, but I feel that if I don't talk to someone soon, I might go over the edge. The pack is having money issues. We've no income coming in right now. Well, very little. The people in the pack, they're having a hard time of it, and I've delayed any dues they might owe to me for a while. But my own bills are mounting up.*

How bad is it? James just lay there, and Rider could see something that he'd not noticed before. James had lost weight. And a great deal of it. *You're suffering, and so is your wolf from worrying about this.*

We all are. I'm not sleeping well. I know that Ruby isn't either. Our own bills are just over five grand. Not a lot compared to some, I guess, but lucky for us the house is paid for and we have no car payment. But other things are beginning to come due. Rider asked him why his pack was having money issues. *Remember that plant that came to town about fifteen years ago? The one that made those specialty boxes for stupid people with pets?*

Yes. They didn't last long. You didn't invest in that, did you?
James said that he'd not had any money to do such a thing.
Then it hit Rider what the problem was. *But your people did.*

*Yes, against my advice. And now that there are people suing
the company for unfulfilled orders, they're being hit hard. I know
that most of them have given up their entire savings to pay them
back. And as you know, while I have a large pack, they're mostly
families with young. Sitters cost money, and so do cars to go out of
town to get jobs.*

I can help you out. James said that's not why he'd told him.
*I know that. Christ, man, you're my friend and I want to help you
out.*

*We need to have a business come to town. That would help
everyone out. I mean, something that will hire a few hundred
people.* Rider thought about that. *The trickle-down theory on
that would help everyone, including you guys.*

*You mean because of the influx of money. You think that the
town would prosper as well.* He nodded. *Do you have any ideas
on what sort of business you think needs to come here? I'm not
without contacts. Perhaps there is a business that is looking for a
place to put a warehouse or something.*

I don't know. He stood up then, and so did Rider. *My mate
calls to me. I need to go back. Thank you, Rider, for letting me vent
to you. I needed that a lot more than I thought. I don't need to tell
you to not tell anyone, do I? I mean, I'd rather not have your family
thinking me a failure.*

No one would think that, James. We've all been there. James
nodded and moved deeper in the woods. *I'm going to look into
that. The business.*

Thank you, but it's all right, Rider. You're a good man. Rider
didn't feel like a good man. Making his way back to the
house, he thought that he was sort of a shit. Smiling, he
wondered how many of his brothers would agree with him.

Now Available in the Lanning's Leap Series

Misha
Lanning's Leap
Book 1

Thomas
Lanning's Leap
Book 2

Carter
Lanning's Leap
Book 3

Phillip
Lanning's Leap
Book 4

Andrew
Lanning's Leap
Book 5

Before You Go...

HELP AN AUTHOR

write a review

THANK YOU!

Share your voice and help guide other readers to these wonderful books. Even if it's only a line or two your reviews help readers discover the author's books so they can continue creating stories that you'll love. Login to your favorite retailer and leave a review. Thank you.

Kathi Barton, winner of the Pinnacle Book Achievement award as well as a best-selling author on Amazon and All Romance books, lives in Nashport, Ohio with her husband Paul. When not creating new worlds and romance, Kathi and her husband enjoy camping and going to auctions. She can also be seen at county fairs with her husband who is an artist and potter.

Her muse, a cross between Jimmy Stewart and Hugh Jackman, brings her stories to life for her readers in a way that has them coming back time and again for more. Her favorite genre is paranormal romance with a great deal of spice. You can visit Kathi on line and drop her an email if you'd like. She loves hearing from her fans. aaronskiss@gmail.com.

Follow Kathi on her blog:
http://kathisbartonauthor.blogspot.com/